BIRMI
Univers

TIMELINES

an anthology

Edited by
Leila Howl, Sophie Owers, Alison Stubbs
and **Andrew Tyers**

Published by twentyfivefiftytwo
for and on behalf of The School of English,
Birmingham City University.

First published 2017
Compilation © The School of English,
Birmingham City University 2017
Contributions © individual copyright holders

This is a work of fiction. Any views, opinions or statements expressed in
this work are those of the individual authors and not the Publisher.

A CIP Catalogue record for this book is available
from the British library

ISBN 978-1-5272-0951-0

Designed and typeset by Mark Bracey

Printed in Great Britain

Contents

Foreword
Kit de Waal

The first time I saw some writing of mine in print it was an unbelievable thrill. I'd entered a competition with a bit of flash fiction and eagerly read the results. My name wasn't on the list of winners, nor on the shortlist, nor on the longlist but right at the bottom there were another ten writers who qualified for an honorary mention. I usually write those words in capitals because it meant so much to me. Honorary Mention!

What is it about publication that means so much to us? Often the fact of publication outweighs the receipt of the prize money – if there is any. Being published, especially in a competitive environment, means that someone somewhere has made an objective assessment of our writing, judged it against others and said 'Yes, this is good.' It means we haven't been working for nothing, sacrificing time and social life, time with our children or partner, knocking our head against the brick wall of our talent and trying to go beyond it. It means that the hours spent alone revising and re-writing and re-reading aloud and endlessly moving commas and full-stops hasn't been for nothing. It means that the thousands we may have paid for courses and books and pens and computers, and turning up for talks and book signings and the craft, oh the craft, none of it was a waste of time. It means we dare to call ourselves writers.

What we have in common is also what sets us apart from one another. We all feel we have something to say and that our something is unique, as yet unwritten or unexpressed. Samuel Taylor Coleridge said 'What comes from the heart, goes to the heart,' and it's clear that the writers in this anthology have written from their hearts to everyone lucky enough to read them. Some have been published before, for others this will be their first time in print. The pieces are wild and clever, sad and funny, all of them well crafted, all of them from the heart. It's a privilege to introduce them to you.

The Taste of Death
Kit de Waal

Emile Boucher chef proprietor, Le Gourmet, Toulouse.

That I should die of cancer of the stomach is entirely appropriate. I eat with my stomach. My stomach eats me. My wife brings me my tray, Boudin sausage, a glass of burgundy, some bread. I enjoy my final meal alone with pen and paper

The recipe for Le Boudin goes thus.

The pigs blood must be fresh. Underline fresh. Fresh blood will keep Le Gourmet open for another two years. Strain for clots. It is spring, the season of sudden change. My wife will contemplate the black linen dress or the woollen skirt. She wants certainties.

Cover and set aside. Chop garlic and onion, sauté in pig fat. After two years, Jean Luc will steal the recipe, as I did and grow rich. Add double cream, cooked rice, wild thyme, rosemary. My wife will be tired by then and will not care. Simmer. The restaurant will close for the funeral, the menu is planned.

Add the blood, stir well, force into hogs casings, poach gently. I ease the tablets deep into the sausage and add by way of a reminder. 'Monique, darling, remember, fresh blood.'

Remove from the heat. Allow to cool.

houston, tx

Rhiannon Fidler

houston, tx

born for the sullen cold
we waited in the ramble
for roots to take hold
and lead us, tangled,
to magnificent worlds.
the spines were waiting,
wild and paralysed,
by the bright fools of the world
in their bittersweet ventures,
all twisting with fear.
and though bruised,
i followed the stream for miles
seeking solace
in the furled forest
and swirling valley.
looking out for when
the ice would kiss the curb
and the creature would bellow
for the hallow to come,
so its tears could melt it away.

houston, tx (reprise)

dawn is blazing
doused in the perfume of a blue night.
wounded spirits rejoice
as the nests begin to thaw.
brighten, quickly,
as moth-winged butterflies rise
away from sweating ground
below
the stashed honey
and its guards are sore.
filling up the fragments
once lost,
now the fiercest memories
of how your darlings have grown.
seduced by swampy lakes
and the first steps of a fawn;
the earth is alive.

demise

the desert's demise
is abundant and lonely,
a drawn out sequence
of romance between sand and rain.
ripped and gnashed
by earth's fingers and teeth,
the stretched land
cries for its former glory.
a burning passion,
a glorious moon,
in celestial conversation
as hollowed eyes take over.
the skulls pretend to care
as the shadows dance across
from the clouds above.
but look! a brook,
a fertile grassland
for tired souls to gaze.
see, the fallow evergreen.
what once was barren populates,
and all that is left is
to move forwards.

My Colony, My Rock
Leila Howl

The storm had bounced off my carapace for hours, but a twitch of my wings shifted most of the debris. The loneliness of the Kalahari was nothing compared to the suffocating silence from my brood sisters' absence. Another twitch dislodged a rock. Coal black, glinting, almost glowing, with that luscious purple-gold that makes your mandibles twitch. It was small enough to hold comfortably, but surprisingly heavy. I forgot my isolation and for a moment found myself wriggling like a larva.

Tucking the rock into the pollen basket on my leg, I went back to my digging. My brood would help process this find when our mind was whole again. It would be worth the wait, to observe it through my sisters' senses, to analyse it thoroughly. But although I knew I should wait, I found myself taking it out, stroking the rough-smooth surface with my antennae. Instead of cursing the emptiness the storm had brought I grew used to it. It seemed to hug me, keeping me safe with my treasure.

No. Our treasure.

I twitched my wings.

Ours. For the colony.

My sisters would be pleased with such a find. What might it do for our status after the next swarming!

But when the storm eased and the air throbbed with their return, I tucked away the rock and went back to my digging.

Usa, the strongest, with a big, drone-like head, spoke aloud. 'We would have come earlier, but you drifted in the storm.' She looked puzzled. 'We felt excitement. Where is your find?'

'It blew away in the winds. I looked, but...' I raised my antennae at the endless Kalahari, lowering my abdomen to echo their disappointment. Only Ninu, the smallest, glanced at me as I tried to still the air rushing through my spiracles.

Usa twitched her wings at my measly piles of dirt. 'We shall search downwind. You continue here.' The brood agreed, and I watched their round abdomens waggle away into the dunes for as long as I could bear before I pulled out the rock.

It was beautiful.

It was mine.

The thought scared me so much I put it away again until my sisters returned, backsides so low their stingers drew paths in the sand.

'It is time to leave,' Usa said. 'Maybe other workers will find it if we continue excavations. We can't risk drifting into a rogue swarm.'

Before she took the lead, Anu, the biggest and fastest, held up her front legs to taste the wind. 'It is odd. The drones seemed so sure there would be a nectar-bed of treasures here, but we have never been anywhere more barren.'

Usa raised her claws. 'The records cannot always be right. The world has changed a lot since they were drawn.'

'True. It is easy to overlook things that our ancestors would have found. Maybe we came to the wrong place.'

'Maybe the drones should check again,' I said.

Ninu clicked her mandibles lightly, but the rest were busy scenting out our dig markers. Once we reached our wide hive tunnels she drew in front of me. 'What was it, Sisi? It felt so beautiful.'

'I couldn't say.' I tried to feel sad.

She paused to look at me.

'You are troubled. We share your sadness. Will we ask to return to the site?'

'I don't know.' The small rock lay heavily in my pouch. The thought of finding more was tempting. But the thought of sharing... I shuddered and quelled the terrifying thoughts.

'At least we obtained sufficient structural information. If we could revegetate, then the swarm could survive here. Imagine this as a forest of flowers!' She waggled on ahead, her dance turning the dark, shrubby sands into fields of clover and nectar until we reached the hive.

The drones were too busy to see us and I was glad to curl up in our cells. I felt the others drift to sleep, until I was the last to close my mind to rest. I was so tired I thought I could sleep through a swarming, yet I woke early, the weight in my leg pulling at my mind.

The brood was peaceful, so I pulled out the rock. It was as beautiful as I remembered. I stroked it, basking in its honey-sweet glow.

'The find!' I had not noticed Ninu wake up. Her surprise woke the others.

'What is this?' Anu asked. 'I thought we returned with empty baskets.' She drew in close, staring at my rock. 'This is the lost find!' Her stinger twitched at me as she stared.

I forced my own stinger to stay low, frightened by my reaction.

'It was in my pollen combs. It...must have stuck to me during the storm.' It did not sound feasible. I held the rock tighter, my whole body ready to twitch. 'I can't explain.'

I could see the thoughts fly between them, their confusion, Ninu's loyalty to me so sweet against Anu's dependence on the proper procedures. Then Usa thrust her big, ugly head in. 'Why are we arguing? We must go to the drones.' She was right, of course. She always was. My sisters agreed.

Anu held out her mandibles towards my rock. 'We must take it.'

'No!' My wings shivered. 'I'll carry it.'

Usa stared at me. 'Let us hear that again.'

I heard myself as if for the first time. 'I...I want to carry it.' I. I was not brood. I was one.

Ninu moved in closer. 'She talks like a queen.'

Usa looked to Anu. 'We cannot feel her thoughts.'

'But she is not dead.'

Maybe I was. Because I realised then, that for the first time since our hatching, I could not feel theirs.

The air vibrated around me as they backed away. Only Ninu stayed close, as the others rushed off to get help.

They sent my sisters to scout without me. The ultimate punishment. Yet, as Ninu's stinger dragged out of sight, their absence didn't tear at my mind as it should have. Guards encased me with wax from stinger to thorax, blocking half my spiracles so I could barely breathe. They carried me through the hive like a corpse. The drones had gathered and the Queen lay in the middle of her cell, fat with eggs, young workers buzzing around, feeding and grooming her constantly. I hadn't seen her since my own days as a carer, but of course she would not remember me from the hundreds that had tended her over the years. She looked older than I remembered, but her scent was still strong and comforting.

A massive drone stared at me with his oversized eyes like I was a naughty grub, before waggling respectfully to her. 'My Queen. We would not normally bother you at such a time, but I fear this matter has interrupted our preparations for the swarm.' She raised her antennae, and he continued. 'Though you are above such things, you of course understand the importance of our brood-mind, my Queen. Without it we may as well regress to a proto-hive, buzzing about the surface day and night in the nectarless days of the human infestation. This one,' he clicked at me rudely, 'is no longer of our swarm.'

The Queen stared at me. 'Did she drift to us?'

'Her egg was of your body.'

Brushing away her attendants she raised her stinger a fraction. 'But the hive does not feel her?'

'She could be dancing in the dark for all we know.'

The stinger twitched. 'Such a one could feed us to the ants.'

'That is true, my Queen. But we fear she is an even greater threat to your regime. There is a buzzing in the air around her. Her unit lacks cohesion, she is lost even to her sisters. She speaks as a Queen, yet she is a worker. The records hold warning of such segregated thinking.' His abdomen was so high he might have already sentenced me. But to what? His arguments seemed winding and pointless, the usual ramblings of an old drone.

The Queen tooted angrily, interrupting him, her stinger now pointed directly at me. 'They said she lied.'

'I'm sorry,' I said.

'She interrupts me!' The Queen piped even louder.

The old drone buzzed softly. 'Something may have infected her mind and she is merely mad. Or there is that more serious concern.' He dropped his abdomen, swaying it meaningfully. 'Either way she should be quarantined for our safety.'

Either what? What concern? 'I'm not mad!' I shouted, looking from Queen to drone and back again, twitching and suffocating in my confinement.

Our eyes met, and she screamed, taking my defence as a challenge. Her wings spread, lifting her from the floor. 'Usurper!' she shouted, a long scream, echoed by three short quacks that made me shiver.

I staggered back as she charged, wings pressed uselessly against my wax prison. The impact was enough to knock me down, fracturing the wax, but not enough to free me. She came at me again, aiming for my body. I rolled, but too slowly. The wax saved me from the worst of her sting, but her blows had been forceful enough to make cracks. A large chunk fell off. At least I could breathe again!

She attacked a third time. I spread my wings and lifted my stinger to meet her. There was no time to be horrified at my actions. Although the thrust pushed her off course, her own stinger penetrated my abdomen. Her venom burned through my body, but still I grappled with her, clawing at her eyes as she pulled my antennae. Shuddering in pain, I lifted my stinger again. The wax had not shattered completely and even as my own venom pooled in readiness, the barbs of my stinger were still coated. That saved my life. Instead of gouging deep into her body and tearing my own in two, I merely scratched her underbelly. But it was enough to make her pull back and scream in my face, her scent angry enough to make my wounded antennae tremble.

As she launched for a final attack, my body spasmed from the poison running through it. I tracked her motion, still, except for an involuntary twitch. As the wind from her wings brushed my own, I dipped and swiped my spurs at her. Breathing was hard again. I panted on the floor, waiting for her final blow. But it didn't come. I dragged my head up to see her huddled across the room, carers coming cautiously to her side. Her hind leg stuck out at an awkward angle, and though she glanced at me, I lay still enough to be little enough of a threat to bother with.

The heat in me became a chill and I lay, twitching, listening to the drones buzzing busily around their wounded but victorious Queen. None came to me, but one buzzed quietly to the guards, and I was re-coated in wax and dragged from the room.

The days after the attack were hot and cold and dark as I fought off the venom. I should have died. At times, I believed I had. But worse than the pain was the loneliness. It was different from the isolation in the desert. Emptier. I buzzed sadly to myself, slowly healing, and used my new mind to call up old memories. My colony. My brood sisters. My rock.

Workers brought me food and helped tend to my wounds. This surprised me at first, especially once I'd decoded the old drone's accusations, and the threat I'd been perceived as. But those scheming, bitter drones spent their lives trying to hide their idleness and impress the Queen and it wouldn't take much for one out of favour to decide that someone new might be useful. The Queen was getting older, and if the leg injury I inflicted damaged her ability to lay, it would not just be drones sacrificed to the Cull this year.

Months passed, until one day Ninu came to feed me. We waggled at each other in happiness but my abdomen stayed low. Isolation had warped my memories so the little Ninu I remembered seemed bigger. I felt as if I had only known her as a pupa. Worst of all, her mind was still severed from mine.

'I didn't think I would ever see you again.' I said.

'Winter is here. The Cull was more violent than ever. They were too busy backstabbing to pay attention to the rota. Here, I thought you would enjoy this for a change.'

Pollen! Slightly fermented, just how I liked it. I waggled more contentedly, nourished, and happier for seeing my little Ninu. Although...

'You will think me mad, but I'm sure you've grown!'

We clicked our mandibles at each other, then she stared at me quietly. 'I thought you would look different by now.'

'They were wrong. Only my mind changed. I'm not growing into a Queen. I kept hoping the drones would come down and notice, but I don't suppose that will happen until spring. Maybe you could tell them?'

She clicked loudly at that. 'Then I would end up here with you!' Looking around, she reached slowly to her leg. 'I found something else amongst the records.'

My rock. It glowed even brighter than I remembered. 'Let me hold it!' I could almost feel it tucked safely against my leg. 'Please, Ninu?'

Her wings twitched. 'No.' She stroked it gently before tucking it back into her pollen sack. 'It's mine.'

Tongues

Shazmeen Khalid

One thick braid slicked back,
That's how my mother arrived in this country.
Baggy kameez hanging over her.
A scarf draped loosely over her head,
With the tail floating off her shoulder.
She brought the smell of Kashmir with her,
She spoke only in its numerous tongues,
And she,
she smiled sweeter than its tea.
That's how she arrived to this country,
Scared and young,
Not familiar with the English tongue.

She is the mother of British children,
Some who lace their lips with mother's verse,
And some who could not learn.
She brought Kashmir with her, my mother did,
And even if I shall never go back -
She raised it inside me.
Bolo. I say to my brothers. Bolo.
Speak.
Speak your mother tongue with grace,
Do not take pride in speaking only
The language of colonisers.
Bolo.

Snails as Pieces
Alex Woodhouse

EXT. PIER

>   Seagulls, calm wind, waves
>   breaking, chess moves.

>   SAL
>   Ok, your move.

>   (beat)
>   Look mate, we don't have any
>   change, alright.

>   PAUL
>   I'm just watching the game.

Chess moves continue.

>   SAL
>   Look, just get lost.

EXT. ALLEYWAY

Heavy rainfall, wind, thunder. A busy street,
pedestrians passing. The soundscape gets closer to
the ground.

Squelches of snails, a bag unzipping and a yawn.

>   SARAH (V/O)
>   I don't think he knows how to play
>   chess. He talks like he does but I
>   don't think he does.

>   SARAH
>   You know how to play chess?

>   PAUL
>   Course.

SARAH
This billboard is doing nothing as
shelter. You slept under this?

PAUL
For a bit. OK, if I have seven of
them and you have seven of them,
then we're even.

SARAH
How do we know which piece is
which?

PAUL
I've got nail polish. We'll mark
'em. One spot for the pawns, two
for the knights, a halo for the
bishop, a crown for the King, a
cross for the Queen.

SARAH
How am I supposed to do a cross on
this shell? It's all cracked.

PAUL
That's why you grab them by the
body.

SARAH
What, and get all the slime on my
hands?

PAUL
I've done it, my hands are fine.

SARAH
Let's see.

PAUL
Nah, you're alright, just keep
painting.

SARAH
Can't. This nail polish is dry as
anything.

                    PAUL
          Press harder then.

                    SARAH
          And pierce through their shells?

                    PAUL
          Wipe it on the damp of the ground
          or try the wall.

Scraping of brush.

                    PAUL (CONT'D)
          Is it working?

                    SARAH
          It's uhh. Not really.

(BEAT)

                    PAUL
          This one's George, and this
          one's... Georgina.

                    SARAH
          Original.

                    PAUL
          Well, what's the name of yours
          then?

                    SARAH
          I'm not naming snails.

                    PAUL
          Go on, just one.

                    SARAH
          Alright, this one is... Bruce.

                    PAUL
          Like Forsyth?

                    SARAH
          I guess so...Yeah. This one is
          Bruce Forsyth.

Fade out sounds of weather.

EXT. STREET

        Fade in sounds of a club from a
        distance, more people walking
        past.

              DRUNKARD
    Here you go.

              SARAH
    Thank you! Have a great night.

              PAUL
    Alright, your move.

              SARAH
    My move? My move? I don't know
    what's happening. You don't know
    what's happening.

              PAUL
    I know what's happening.

              SARAH
    Paul, a world champion couldn't
    figure out what's happening here.
    The pizza box is covered in snail
    gunk, the nail polish has come off,
    I can't see anything for this chip
    shop's neon sign.

              PAUL
    It's not that bad.

              SARAH
    That one's a slug, how did a slug
    get in here!

(BEAT)

A lairy crowd of women walking past, high heels
and bellowing sounds of drunken laughter.

              PAUL
    Oh great.

                    SARAH
          It's alright, it's alright.

                    KAREN
          Oi! Got the time.
                    (Laughs)

                    SARAH
                    (Hushed)
          They'll be gone, it's alright.

                    KAREN
          Oi.

                    PAUL
          Hey, can you just get lost.

                    KAREN
          You what?

                    SARAH
          Nothing. Nothing.

                    KAREN
          Nah, what did you say?

                    SARAH
          Please.

                    SAMANTHA
          Oi Karen, come on.

                    KAREN
          On my way. What are you two doing?

                    SARAH
          Nothing.

                    KAREN
          Oi Sam, get over here.

Heels clicking.

                    SAMANTHA
          What? Ugh, what's this?

>   SARAH
> Nothing.

>   KAREN
> It looks like you're playing with
> slugs. Is that what you're doing?

>   PAUL
> For your information, these are
> snails, now leave us b-

The squelching creeps into the soundscape.

>   KAREN
> Ugh. There's one going up your
> shoe Sam, Kill it!

Screams of shock from the women. Heels hitting,
shells cracking. Squelches turn to squeals.

>   PAUL
> No! Not Bruce!

>   SAMANTHA
> Let's get out of here.

KAREN and SAMANTHA walk away.

(BEAT)

Paul sobbing.

>   PAUL
> They killed Bruce Forsyth.

>   SARAH
> How do you know it was Sir Bruce?

>   PAUL
> Because of the markings, see?

>   SARAH
> I'm not gonna lie, it just looks
> like slime to me.

>   PAUL
> Well it's him, and we need to
> commemorate him.

                  SARAH
       Yeah sure.

                  (BEAT)
       Oh what, right now? Erm, I'm
       really sad about your death and
       you were a good pawn and...
       friend? Yeah.

                  PAUL
       Good night, sweet prince.

PAUL starts to murmur *In the Arms of an Angel*.
A siren goes off in the distance, fade out.

EXT. PIER

Fade in seagulls, a bus going past. Slow squelch.

                  PEDESTRIAN
       Here you go mate.

Sound of change.

                  PAUL
       Have a great day.

                  (beat)
       Sarah. Sarah.

                  SARAH
                  (Yawning)
       What? You're-

She is suddenly awakened.

                  SARAH (CONT'D)
       Jesus Christ!

Squelch.

                  PAUL
       Calm down, it's only a snail.

       Thirteen more and we're set for
       another game.

                    SARAH
Well have you learnt how to play?

                    PAUL
I'm just fine. I know how to play
chess.

                    SARAH (V/O)
I don't think he knows how to play
chess.

06:59 to Milton Keynes Central

Kate Aspinall

We stand in clumps
carriage spaced,
each plugged in
to soundscapes, placed
in empty ears
on busy heads
that left cold wives
in clean warm beds.

We are sorry to announce –

In dry cleaned uniformity
over-toeing the yellow line
we experts look
up from our apps
set down our bags
and look
up through the gaps
in our synapses packed
with the data we need for the breach.

The next train to arrive will be the delayed –

Brows crumple to communicate the daily irk,
a validation of us against
the tick-tock-tick of un-waiting work.

Our minute by minute importance plumes as pollution in
our chests.

The train now arriving at Platform 2 –

The approach
lifts our chins
perpendicular
to the platform

our synapses packed
with the data we need for the breach.

The Prosecution

Joe Legge

I

The Prosecution approached the Accused, who had placed one hand on the cover of the King James Bible. In a voice flattened by repetition, the Prosecution said, 'Do you swear to tell the truth, the whole truth, and nothing but the truth so help you-'. There was a murmur from somewhere in the crowded courthouse. The Prosecution cleared his throat. '-so help you God?'

And God said, 'Yes, I do.'

'Good,' said the Prosecution. He went back to his desk and looked at a blank piece of paper and collected his thoughts while pretending to review his notes. 'Where were you' he said, 'on the morning of the 23rd of January this year?'

God took a sip of water and leaned toward the little micro-phone. 'In the beginning, I created the heavens and the earth. And the earth was without form, and void; and darkness was-'. The Prosecution furrowed his brow and looked to the Judge who nodded.

'Where is this going?' the Judge said to God.

'To the apocalypse, your honour,' said God.

'Excuse me?'

'The end of the world?'

The Judge frowned at God. 'And why are you telling us this?'

'It's the whole truth, your honour.'

'Ah,' the Judge said, 'While your obedience is much appreciated I would ask you to keep your testimony to the facts of the case.'

'Yes, your honour,' God said and tried to laugh off His mistake.

'What was the question again?'

The Prosecution repeated himself.

'Oh yes! The 23rd?' God thought for a moment. 'I believe I was with you.'

The Prosecution's mouth fell open. In twenty years of criminal law he had never heard a reply so ridiculous.

'I assure you that I am quite certain you were not with me.'

'I was with you,' God said and smiled. 'I was with the Judge too.'

The Judge rubbed his chin and the Prosecution's left eye twitched as he pretended to look at his notes again. 'The Judge and I,' he said, 'were not together on the 23rd. You could not have been with the pair of us so would you like to consider your answer again?'

'Certainly.' God said. 'What I meant was that I was *in* you. You and the Judge.'

The Judge had a small coughing fit and the Prosecution's face turned red.

'Oh dear,' God said, 'there seems to have been another misunderstanding. You see, I am above all things, through all things, and in all things, including you.' He smiled again.

The Prosecution realised that any specificity was going to have to come from him, rather than Him. 'On the 23rd of January forty-seven people – most of them children – died when a sinkhole opened up and caused their school to collapse in on them.' The Prosecution took a breath. 'Were you there?'

'Yes,' God said, leaning back in His chair.

'And what were you doing there?'

'I was just,' He shrugged, 'watching.'

'Watching?'

'That's right.'

'And did you enjoy watching?'

God raised His eyebrows. 'I suppose I did, actually. I've never thought about it like that.'

'So,' the Prosecution said, 'you became aware of this disaster as it was unfolding and rushed to see it?'

'No, I was already there, and everywhere.'

'You knew that this was going to happen?'

'Indeed.'

The Prosecution picked up a brown folder from his desk. 'Tell me,' he said 'did you make the school collapse?'

In the minutes preceding this question there were occasional sounds from the congregation; a whisper, a cough, the turn of a notebook page, and the clicking of expensive pens. Now there was cold silence.

God shifted in his seat. 'Well, you see, I wouldn't want to...I wouldn't say it quite like that.'

The Prosecution looked at Him for a beat and approached Him with the folder open. He handed it to God and spoke to the entire room.

'This is the official report of the incident: the professional opinions of all the heads of the emergency services involved, as well as geological consultants, engineering consultants, and the coroner.' Turning back to God he said 'Would you please read aloud the highlighted part of these experts' report?'

God cleared His throat. 'This investigation concludes that neither the School Board nor the City is at fault in this tragic incident. It was an... It was an act of God.'

The Prosecution spoke louder, 'Could you read that last bit again, please?'

God's head hung down as he repeated the words, 'It was an Act of God.'

The Prosecution took back the brown folder. 'Do you believe the conclusion of these several experts to be wrong?'

God sat up straight and almost knocked over his water glass.

'No, but I'd like to-'

'So you agree with the report?'

There was a long pause in which the Prosecution's eyes narrowed.

'Yes,' God said.

'You confess that you caused the school to collapse knowing that forty-seven people would die?'

God looked at his hands and spoke quietly. 'Yes.'

'In our society we call that murder.'

'No!' God protested, 'I didn't murder them, well, technically… but it wasn't like that, I was bringing them home. They're at peace, I promise.'

The Prosecution was expecting this.

'Your motives do not excuse your crimes. The facts are simple: you carried out premeditated murder and must pay your debt to society.' Then, addressing the Judge, 'I would like to recommend the strictest sentence.'

II

There was a fifteen-minute recess for the Defence to prepare for his examination. God returned to His seat in the witness box, swore to tell the truth, the whole truth and nothing but the truth. He took a sip of water. The Defence stood and spoke to his client.

'Just to clarify, you don't deny doing what it is that you have been accused of doing on January 23rd?'

'No, I don't deny it,' God said, His head up, sitting straight once again.

'Do you understand the consequences of your actions?'

'Indeed I do, better than most.'

'And do you see your actions as morally wrong?'

'I don't think there's anything wrong with what I've done.'

'Would you be so kind as to explain how your actions of the 23rd can be justified? Why you did what you did and so forth?'

'In My position, I have the responsibility and honour of escorting My beloved children back into My presence. On the 23rd I was merely carrying out that responsibility once more.'

'And can you tell us,' the Defence asked, 'are those forty-seven people,' he paused and glanced at the Jury, 'are they happy?'

'I promise that they are.' God smiled, His eyes became shiny.

'Thank you.' The Defence said, and then, turning to address the courtroom, 'It would appear that my client was simply doing his duty as God. It seems that He has always done it, and what's more important is that the *so-called victims* in this *alleged* crime are perfectly happy. I reason that this case be dismissed and all charges against God be dropped.'

The Defence sat down and looked at God who smiled back at him. They nodded to each other; it had been exactly planned. The question of morality, the prickliest topic for a sensitive Jury, was dealt with.

The Judge invited a response from the Prosecution who stood up, buttoned his suit jacket, and paced a line from one end of the Jury box to the other and back again.

'Your honour,' the Prosecution said, 'I understand that death is a natural part of life. I'm sure everyone in this room realises that. But this is not a place where we discuss what is natural. It is not even necessary for us to wax philosophical about the meaning of morality. We are in a court of law. Whatever your religious beliefs, your moral code or private prejudices, if you are in this country you are subject to its laws. If you break the law you must pay your debt to society. There has been no debate of the facts of the case: the Accused intentionally caused the death of forty-seven people. In this country we call that murder, or to be more specific, He is a *mass*-murderer.'

An uncomfortable rumble was heard from the audience. The Prosecution was familiar with uncomfortable rumbles and felt that this was a good sign.

He continued.

'The Accused has pleaded guilty and shown no remorse. Let's think about the children He freely admits to murdering. Their parents deserve justice!' And he stretched out his hand in the direction of the crying men and women in the front pews of the court. 'Is it not our duty as a society to hold ourselves and our citizens to a standard higher than that which the Accused has displayed? Nobody is above the law. Once again, I ask the court to find the Accused guilty on forty-seven counts of pre-meditated murder because that is the truth. As jurors, it is your responsibility to ensure that this mass-murderer does not walk free today.'

The rumble sounded calmer now. The Prosecution knew he had won.

III

This would be a landmark case. The Prosecution would be famous. He could get a prestigious job in any firm, teach at any university, and write articles or books about this case. He could retire as a rich man and while away his final years enjoying the profits that come from this ruling. He could buy some new clubs and finally get his handicap down. He could buy a boat and find out if he liked fishing. And his life would come to a peaceful end in a private hospital room with the very best of medical care. His legal legacy was confirmed in the sound of that rumble. All he had to do was sit and be patient until the guilty verdict came back. His stiff back had started to feel less stiff.

The Judge dismissed the Jury to make their deliberations. The Prosecution began to gather papers and put them in his brief-case. He imagined television and newspaper interviews. Maybe a movie would be made about him. By the magic of cinema, he could become immortal.

He clipped shut his case. God looked over at him and caught his eye. Surely the Accused, surely God, wouldn't hold a grudge. He was, of course, only doing his job, and doing it very well. There was no sin in that. But what about after retirement? Standing outside the pearly gates perhaps wouldn't be a comfortable place to be when St. Peter read the great ledger of life. The Man Who Jailed God would be unlikely to win many friends in heaven. But he certainly wouldn't be happier in hell. The weight was lowering itself back onto his shoulders.

The smile faded from the Prosecutor's lips and his eyes stared at nothing as he contemplated his fate. To jail God would be damnation and yet he was sure that he had convinced the Jury it was the right thing to do. The Jury! It was in their hands, and one of them must realise what a guilty verdict would mean for him, and possibly for the Jury too. They hadn't spent the last three months using every drop of energy to compile a case against The Almighty. They had been sitting in a courtroom for hours, dozens of hours, in the same room as God which means they had the perfect opportunity to think calmly about Him. He hadn't had a second to consider his soul. That is the only way out. The Jury finds Him innocent, the Prosecutor goes on with his life, and when he gets to heaven he and God have a no-hard-feelings kind of conversation and shake hands.

Hopefully, the Jury won't take long.

11:11pm

Sophie Ludgate

DOA

The world ends in fire.

Red and gold and yellow and orange.

And loud. Crackling, crackling, crackling. Roaring, louder than the beat in my eardrums. And there are people, people everywhere. I can't move I can't get them out. I can't save them.

Tommy, Ed, Harry. Lizzie, Emily, Cass, Mona.

The fire, it consumes them. All of them. One by one I see them disappear into the red and gold and yellow and orange.

It's majestic, mighty, magnificent.

It's furious, raging, deadly.

It's taking the people I love. Not me.

Crackling, crackling, crackling.

All around me. Everywhere. But it won't consume me, won't take me to my friends. It dances closer but not close enough. It's playing with me like a child playing acky; gaining, dodging, taunting. It reaches out a hand but when I try to take hold, it pulls back and laughs.

It calls my name. 'Alice...Alice...Alice...'

Just Breathe

'Alice! Alice, wake up.' I open my eyes and see Cassie's frantic fingers pinching my cheeks, tapping my sore flesh. She sighs. 'Jesus, Ali.' I look around. Everyone's okay. Thank fuck.

'Oh my god, what just happened?'

Cassie laughs. 'You. Your fucking maniac driving.' Shit. 'You saved us.'

I did what? My belt is jammed, so I rummage through my bag for my penknife. Cassie is still singing my praises to the others; they're all huddled and excited, happy to be alive. I grab my knife and the light in the car changes.

'Oh my god, get out. Get out of the car!'

Cassie looks at me, confused, but Emily has seen them: headlights. 'Shit! Cass open the door!'

Cassie looks at me, they all do.

'GET THE FUCK OUT OF THE CAR!' I start sawing at my belt, knowing damned well I don't stand a chance.

Cassie opens the door but it's too late, far too late.

There's not even time to scream.

Run

The world is white, like a blank sheet of paper. White is the colour of hospitals, mental institutions, morgues. It's supposed to be comforting. White is the colour of the future; smartphones, tablets, cars. Technology is white but it's cold and scary.

I have so much space, but I feel trapped in this white world.

Something cold hits my nose, and the feeling spreads. It's snowing. Explains the white. For the first time, I wonder where I am and how long I've been here. It wasn't snowing before.

Before what?

I don't know.

So I walk. Got nothing better to do.

I walk until my legs ache and breathing burns and then walk some more.

Because something is following me. I see it in the corner of my eye but when I turn around there is nothing there. I try to surprise it, walk a mile or so without looking and then I turn around, but no, there's nothing there.

'Alice…Alice.'

My legs ache and breathing burns but I run, fast, faster. I feel like I'm going to faint.

'Alice.'

Fuck no.

'It's all your fault, Alice.'

I know it is.

'They're all gone because of you, Alice.'

I know.

'You don't deserve to live, Alice.'

God damn it, I know.

But still, I run.

I See Fire

I wake up and I scream and scream because, fuck, how can anything hurt this much, so I scream and scream and then I stop.

I'm in an ambulance. I can see the St. John's sticker on the window.

It doesn't hurt.

Then I see fire.

Everybody dies.

Wires

'Alice. Come on baby.'

'Mr Wallace, you know the rules.'

'I promised her I'd stay with her.'

'Where she is, she doesn't know the difference.'

'The doc said there was brain activity.'

'Sporadic. If she's in there, she's hiding.'

'Wouldn't you? She needs to know that it weren't her fault.'

'You think she knows what happened?'

'She knows. That's why you won't wake up, isn't it baby? But it weren't your fault, okay?'

'Public visiting hours are over, Mr Wallace.'

'Do you see her family here? I can't leave her. She'll be alone. She needs to be reminded she isn't alone.'

'Okay Mr Wallace, five more minutes.'

A door opens with a snick, and closes with a bang.

'Happy, princess? I just cried in front of a nurse. Now that was your fault. If you'd just open them gorgeous eyes and call me a pussy, everything'd be nifty.'

'Hey, any news?'

'Careful, Nurse Happy's on the prowl.'

'Won't stay long mate. Just wanted to see her. Can't even imagine...'

'I need her to wake up. Don't know what to do if she don't. But...what if she does wake up?'

'If she does wake up we'll accept it for the miracle it is and help her through it. All of us. You good with that?'

'You asking if I'll break again? She's the only one who noticed, man. Or at least, the only one who did anything about it. Who knows where the fuck I'd be without her. In fact, no. I know where I'd be, dead or rotting in a jail cell somewhere.'

'So why'd you tell her you hated her?'

'God, she told you that? At the time I guess I did. Needed the drugs more than I needed her. Right now I can't believe that was ever true. I'd give anything for her to wake up, man.'

'I know. Me too. Just keep talking to her. Let her know she isn't to blame. You know she's in there, she's too damn stubborn not to be. Aren't you chick? Want anything to eat?'

'Nah mate you're alright.'

A door opens with a snick, and closes with a bang.

'See? It's not just me babe. Even Harry don't blame you. We all want you to wake up. Need you to wake up. It's no one's fault. Just one of them things. Cassie's folks have been by. Don't know if you heard them. Don't know if you're hearing me. If you are, baby, then listen and listen good. No one fucking blames you. I don't, the lads don't, the girls wouldn't. Even the fuckin' Daily Mail don't blame you. That truck driver, they've finally found out who he is. He'd been on the road for fifteen hours or some-thing stupid like that. If anyone, he's the one to blame. Well, him...the society who made him think working seventeen hours a day was acceptable...'

'God, why won't you wake up? I'm not even fucking religious, why do I keep saying that? Maybe it'll help. Nah. Probably not. Save that for when I get proper desperate. Because I will. You're the reason I got clean. The least you could do is wake the fuck up.'

'If it's because you're scared, I'll tell you the same words you told me a thousand times.

Stop being a pussy.'

Yellow Submarine

It's trying to corner me, guilt me into giving up. I'm leaning against something cold. I can't see anything, but I can hear metal clanging, getting faster, louder. It's chasing me again.

So I run through the darkness, stumbling, crashing into hard metal walls. Where the hell am I?

It's cold. Smells like mould and salt. I don't know where I am.

I see it, in the corner of my eye.

Always in the corner of my eye. I run and I run. I'm going in fucking circles. No I'm not. I see a perfect rectangle of light. A door. A fucking door.

It's not locked, but– salt.

There's water, for miles. I'm on a boat. Of course I am. Mould and salt. The ocean is deep and dark, pulling me in like a vacuum. I'm thrilled and terrified. I'm shaking.

Help me.

Who?

God, no one's coming. I'm all alone.

I'm standing, frozen, staring at the deep dark.

'Alice.'

Stop being a pussy.
I fall.

Life
It hurts. People come and go in waves, drifting in and out. You're always with me, holding my hand, stroking my hair. You refuse to leave me even when the doctors tell you to. When you needed me I sent you away but here you are, looking after me when I need you. You still rarely leave my side and that's good. You keep my mind busy.

Thank you.

You're helping. I can't tell you this, but you are.

You saved me.

I can't wake up, but I'm here now. I'm here for you. I will open my eyes. I will look at you and you'll laugh and smile and however briefly, we'll be happy.

There will be an aftermath. It won't be pretty. But know this – I chose life. I chose life for you, for me, for those we've lost and those we've yet to gain.

Just maybe remind me of that once in a while.

I can hear you again. Praying. But you were never religious. Maybe I should be now. I don't know if I've had a religious experience. I don't think so. I felt a connection, a oneness, but there were no pearly gates.

You're asking me to wake up and believe me I'm trying.

I'm worried about judgment, about facing those who practically raised me. I killed their kids. It wasn't my fault they died, but I was driving. I should have done something but I didn't. But I chose life so that is something I am going to have to deal with. I have to face my own parents too. I haven't heard their voices. I guess it makes sense. Maybe one day they'll forgive me.

I will wake up. In the meantime, think of our future. We'll get there.

I was thinking about you. I always think about you.

It's my fault. It's your fault. It's my fault.

It's his fault.

It's no one's fault

Just one of those things.

Right.

But – I chose life.

I'll forever be remembering and imagining. But they don't blame me.

You don't blame me.

That's enough for now.

Float

Junction thirteen. Twelve. Eleven. Which one did I just drive past? God it's been a long day. Twelve hours now. No, fourteen. Something like that.

Fuck I'm tired.

Breaking the law, again. Not that the gaffer cares. The hard shoulder looks so tempting.

'TIREDNESS CAN KILL TAKE A BREAK'

Easy for you to say.

Nah, cold air and loud music is all I need.

So many times it happens too fast, you change your passion for glory.

Who needs sleep?

Oh shit, veering a bit there.

I can just make out an obscene gesture through the window of the Micra, but the driver doesn't beep the horn. Isn't reflex yet, obviously. Don't worry pet, one day it will be.

Oh man, I'm tired.

Don't know why I'm hurrying. I won't get fired, and I got nowt to get home for. Absolutely nowt.

No, I have to get to Dover by 4 o'clock.

I HAVE to get to Dover by 4 o'clock.

But, fuck, I'm tired.

I could stop.
What time is it?
Shit

Fairy-tales and Castles
'Mommy, how long?'
  'Shush, just go to sleep sweetie.'
  I not tired. I tell her but she don't hear.
  I like when we played I Spy but she don't like it for long. Nor Daddy. They say shush, just go to sleep sweetie.
  Mmm, sweeties. 'Mommy, Skittle.'
  'No, darling, you need to go to sleep.'
  No. Sleep's for babies. Not a baby, Miss told me.
  Mommy says I'm not gonna see Miss for 8 days. Or Emily or Jessie. That's long. They're my friends. We play tig. I wanna play tig.
  I poke Benji. He's funny. Not moving though. Benji sleeping. He's not a baby.
  I don't wanna sleep. I wanna see Mickey and Minnie and Goofy. They're funny.
  Mommy says I can be a princess like Cinderella. She's pretty. I wanna be a pretty princess.
  'Mommy, will you be a princess too?'
  'Yes baby, we'll be princesses together.' Yay, me and Mommy both as princesses. 'Come on Ellie, go to sleep. You don't wanna be tired when we get there, do you?'
  Daddy whispers something to Mommy and it makes her smile. He makes her smile a lot. He's funny too.
  'Okay then Ellie.' She turns around and that smile is for me now. *'You'll remember me when the west wind moves, upon the fields of barley.'*

From Where You Are

Christ, an hour in the car already, how are they not tired yet? It's like having kids. I imagine.

Laughing and talking and shouting and laughing. Which is fine, we're all mates. They're just excited. But, hello, I am trying to drive guys, just sayin'."

Fuck sake.

We put three sugars in our tea, sit to watch day time T.V and laugh at mums who don't know who the father is.

Love this song. Reminds me of you. That's probably weird. Can't wait to see you. Neither can the others. They still don't know about us. I'm proper nervous. How are you gonna act? How should I act?

Gah, they don't even know we were together, the four people I trust most, and we're driving to see you and I have to act like the summer didn't happen.

Fuck you.

So what's the point in getting your hopes up when all you're ever getting is choked up?

Hate this one. Reminds me of you. Why we finished. Still remember you drunk, again, shouting, desperate for my forgiveness. Tough shit, sunshine.

Wonder how you're getting on. Hope you're clean mate, I really do.

But it's over. Has to be. We're bad for each other.

Yep. Totally sticking to me guns. Over.

Fuck that.

Well grey clouds wrapped round the town like elastic, cars stood like toys made of Taiwanese plastic. The boy laughed at the spastic dancing around in the rain.

Reminds me of all the times we went dancing, me and you. Walking through town in the middle of the night, laughing at all the stiffs, all the sluts, all the freshers. Damn we had some good times, mate, right?

Grinding and drinking and laughing and going back to yours, or mine if the folks were out. Yeah, it was a good summer.

Pity you had to ruin it.

'Oh fuck' Squeals and groans as I swerve away from the piss-shead driving the bleeding lorry about to crush Penny. 'Watch me fockin' car, you wanker!'

A chorus of angry shouting, every swear word known to man.

I smile. Yeah.

Fuck you.

At least they're singing now, not nattering away. Less things to try and concentrate on.

I look at the clock. 11:11pm.

Fuck.

Mackerel for Tea

Rhoda Greaves

Bubbles explode on the surface, like someone's dipped in a massive straw and blown a storm into the lemonadey waters.

'Look!' shouts Joe, pointing out to sea. And we see it too – a whole shoal of mackerel tangled in silver chains. There are heaving lines everywhere, with two, three, even four fish latched on at a time, and fishermen up and down the shoreline all shouting to each other, and struggling to pull them in.

'Here, catch hold.' As Joe turns to me his hands are almost ripped from his rod. We dig our wellies into the shingle and have to drag it in together and dump the wriggling fish on the beach. Joe passes Dad's old blue bucket to Finn: 'Can you fill it up?' he says, and Finn edges towards the water. As he jabs the rim into the sea, a small wave breaks over his ankles. He squeals and drops the bucket: yanks off his wet jelly shoes and holds them over his head to let the cold seawater escape from the toe-holes.

'Get it, Sassy,' says Joe and I grab the bucket before it's dragged out with the wave. I have to rinse out the tiny pebbles first, then I can fill it with water. Joe casts outs again and we keep well back like Dad taught us. Once, when Joe was just learning to fish, his hook flicked backwards and stuck in my hair. And I screamed and screamed even though Dad tried to be gentle when he cut it out with his fishing scissors. He called me his brave princess. Said thank God it wasn't my cheek or something even worse. Now, every time Joe's rod swings out, I try not to imagine my bleeding eye squelched on the end of it, unable to shut out the water before it plunges into the sea.

We stand silently for a few moments, even Finn, who can't usually stand still for a second, and watch the waves zigzag with hundreds of metal stripes. There's another tug on Joe's line and he snaps it up to show us a new bunch of fish. Then, after a few minutes, he gets a bite again.

'It's too easy,' Joe says. 'There must be some sea bass chasing them in. You okay to cut one of these mackerel into bait strips for me?'

'Course,' I say.

Mum says me and Finn have to do what Joe says as he's in charge now. Joe's fifteen, so he's been on his own loads, but we could go this time, only if we promised to stay out of the sea: mainly Finn, who's only five so he hasn't learnt to swim yet. I've got nearly all my swimming badges already, and Joe didn't get all his until he was twelve. No one can tell when the rip tide is going to reach in and suck you under. And we are precious. That's what Mum says.

'Just grab my filleting knife,' Joe tells me. 'I put it in the picnic bag, okay?'

'Come on, Finny,' I say, and Finn tries to lift the bucket of fish but it's much too heavy for his little hands. I grab the handle and straighten up tall like the big fat *World's Strongest Man* on the telly at Christmas time. I grit my teeth, a bit in pain like him too, but only when my back is turned away from Joe.

Sometimes, it's hard to remember your spot so you have to look out for landmarks. Cars are parked to the far left and the three white farmhouses should be on our right. It looks like they're squashed into the hillside so they can't slip off and tumble into the sea. When the shingle starts turning to sand we see our picnic blanket next to a clump of scruffy weeds with tiny yellow flowers right in the middle. Finn runs and jumps on it like it's a PE mat at school.

'Don't get it sandy,' I say. And a woman with a big Andrex dog smiles at me as she walks past. I watch her footprints flicking up sand as they edge away. A family is playing cricket and she shouts at the dog to stop spoiling their game. There's hardly ever anyone here except for people fishing. Mum says it's because there's no ice-cream man and no life-guards, and the loos are full of flies.

The fish flop and slop in their bucket when I set it down, but Finn guards them so they can't escape while I feel around for a weapon, picking out the blackest stone I can find. I lift it then and bang it on the sand to practice my aim. It leaves a fish-sized mark. The bucket shimmers with eely movements and I wrap my hand around the first fish I can get hold of. It slithers away, too quick for me, so I go in again more firm this time and throw a slippery body out of the bucket and on to the sand. It leaps and makes to slide away from me, so I giggle and grab it. With Finn watching on I take the fish in my left hand and pick up the sharp rock with my other, stretching back my arm like Robin Hood about to fire his dead-straight arrow, but my hand just drops to the floor.

'What's wrong, Sassy,' says Finn.

But before I can change my mind about the killing I catch sight of Joe casting his line and staring out over the water: Mum would have said he looks just like Dad. I raise my arm again and force my hand down. Bash the fish in its face. It flip-flaps a dance, its gills opening and closing like your mouth under water when you dive too deep and have to kick hard for the surface. I pull away, and though my hand is shaking, I lift the rock again and whack the fish. Whack it. Its life spits in my face. I bring down my arm again and again, again and again: enough for the dark sticky blood to dirty the beach. Enough to stop the fish from fighting for its life. Enough to stop it doing its crazy dance of death. I close my eyes then, even though it doesn't stop me seeing. I don't want to open them up to Finn in case I might want to smash him up too.

A stink makes its way up my nose and I peep out, swallowing

a mouthful of sick. Finn is looking at me, his eyes glittering like the flashes of silver Joe attached to his rod to attract the mackerel. As he leans towards me, I see that his cheeks are wet. He puts out his finger and strokes the twitching fish. It's all over.

'Why did he die, Sassy?' a little voice asks me.

'Because he was brave,' is all I can whisper, repeating what Mum told me last year: she would have been proud of how I said it. I wipe a tear from his face, leaving a line of fishy blood that smudges across his cheek like war paint. The zip of the bag jams and I have to work it backwards and forwards a few times to release it. I'm careful with Joe's knife, and gently slit the silky underneath of the fish.

'Do you want to do it?' I hold it open, hoping Finn wants to do the gory guts that he used to call the glory guts. He shakes his head even though he's helped before, so I scoop out its bloody insides before cutting off the head and tail and slicing off a few stupid pieces that look nothing like the neat fillets Dad would have done.

'Here, take these to Joe.'

Finn pulls away from me, and shakes his head.

'Stay here then.' I run from him, down to the water.

'Thanks,' Joe says as I hold out my hand. He looks at me, and we both look at the jagged meaty chunks. He doesn't take the mick; doesn't even turn up his nose. Just nods me away. And I swish my hands in the sea and scrub at them with sand. I scrub them. Scrub them again.

I go back to Finn and he's sitting, eyes closed, hands together: the rest of the fish's body is gone.

'What are you doing?'

'Shush, Sassy. I'm praying. Help me get some stones and we can make a cross for his grave.'

I don't say anything. Just get the best I can find. Large grey stones that you're not supposed to take home from the beach as they are there to stop the sea from escaping. Dad once told me people do anyway; fill up their carrier bags and use them for ornaments: pile them high in great glass jars. I empty the collection next to the pile of sand where Finn's buried the fish, and help him mark the grave with Jesus's sign. We pray together, the special one that begins *Our Father*, then both our eyes grow tears. Finn wants to empty out the rest of the fish into the water, but I tell him we can't: Mum will be proud of our catch and cook up a treat for us all.

I pull a pack of Jammy Dodgers from the bottom of the picnic rucksack and pour us both a hot cup of tea that Mum did us in a flask. We dip our tongues into the soft red jelly in the middle of our biscuits and lick the heart-shaped holes clean. Then we play in the sand for a bit, and Finn helps me make a sand angel. I read him his favourite book *The Big Honey Hunt* that he's had from when he was small.

Joe comes back and when he sees Finn's book he does a good impression of smart old papa bear trying to get the honey. Then Joe has to read it to him: I don't think he will, but Finn looks like he's about to cry again so Joe gives in easily. I lie back in the sand and listen to the story even though it's supposed to be for little kids.

Joe didn't get as much as a sniff at the sea bass, but there's so much mackerel he's had to borrow extra buckets. When we get home we take some round to the neighbours and the vicar and his wife at the vicarage at the end of our road. You should have seen Mum's face, all bright and beautiful. She doesn't get to cook this kind of thing often, hardly ever. Money's precious, she always tells us, even with Dad's pension. And that has to see us all the way to the future.

She used to cook posh stuff all the time when Dad was on leave. We had to go up to bed early and be as quiet as mice while their friends were round for dinner: big men and their chubby wives. She always let us leave the telly on as long as we liked, only if we kept the volume down. Mum would drink too much wine and get all giggly. Not spiky like some of the others, just slurry and shiny. We all loved those evenings as she always brought us up hot chocolate and a little taster of each of their desserts, shushing us with a red-polished fingernail to her lips, kissing us gently. Pressing a heart of lipstick on our heads. Leaving her own party smell; perfume, wine and maybe one or two cigarettes. Cigarettes are her only perfume now.

Mum reaches up to the high shelves in the kitchen and walks her fingers along the edges of the cookbooks until she gets to the one she wants. While we carefully pack the mackerel into the bottom of the fridge so it doesn't leak its blood over the cheese and yogurts, she pulls a heavy book into her hands and gets straight to the pages she needs.

'Ah,' she says, reading and sniffing our imaginary dinner, 'pan-fried mackerel with orange and harissa, peppered mackerel fish cakes, barbecued mackerel with ginger, chilli and lime drizzle . . .' she closes the cookbook but carries on, 'or simply foil-wrapped with olive oil and garlic and a twig or two of fresh rosemary from the garden.' She kisses her fingers and blows. Finn claps to catch a kiss then starts up his tears again. Mum lifts him up even though he's heavy now.

'What is it, baby boy. What's wrong?' She rubs gently at the stinking stain on his cheek.

'Mummy,' he whispers.

'Yes, my darling, what is it?'

'It's the dead ones.'

Joe shudders. No one wants to upset Mum.

'What?' she says, frowning, lowering Finn to the floor.

'Don't make me eat them.'

A dead fish swims into my mind; its eyes glassy and unblinking.

'Please.' Finn tries out his cutest grin. '*Please.* Can't we just go to the chippy and get normal fish and chips instead?'

Mum goes to say something but it turns into a giggle. I start too. Even Joe joins in a bit. I giggle so hard my nose runs. So hard I might never stop.

Finn wraps himself in Mum's Indian cotton skirt, and its tiny silver bells jangle against his hair as he tries to hide his face.

Mum hugs him even closer: 'Why not?' she says, her hair bobbing round the curl of her smile. 'Why ever not? Normal fish and chips it is!' she laughs.

Feather

Paris McCalla

The feather of a carcass is rugged and uncivilized.

Split, bloodied and plucked

from a body.

Emancipated. Separated. Pulled out of life

but beautiful and light,

floating horizontally.

These soft reminders emerge subtly as lost feathers

and are left behind whilst hunting

as a hobby.

Scoop of the Centuries
Steve McFall

I didn't think my jaw was broken. I ran my finger along it and the bone was smooth enough but the skin was torn and bleeding. My hands weren't bound so I tore a sleeve off my frock and pressed it to my chin. I noticed that at some point during my arrest, I must have lost one of my earrings, although I realised that this would soon be the least of my problems. They had chained my ankle to the damp limestone wall, just as they had with De Winter but he was already dead. His body was now slumped in the corner of the dark chamber with his lifeless face lit by a glowing brazier.

I heard voices, saw shadows, and then the guards re-entered. The biggest and most vicious of the pair shoved a smoky, spitting torch into the loose masonry. The other prisoner was on the rack and the smaller guard didn't waste any time in giving the oak spindle a quarter turn. There was a jolting and shaking as the machine pulled ligaments and sinews to snapping point. The prisoner was cut free and fell onto the granite floor, landing on all fours. A hefty leather boot kicked him full in the rib cage and he dropped onto his side. The same guard then dragged him by his hair to a desk by a stone staircase. A grubby pair of hands placed a document in front of the prisoner and forced a quill into his twisted claw. He started to write a meandering signature, but he wasn't doing it quickly enough for the large guard who produced a knife. He stabbed him in the back of the hand in a strange effort to make him scrawl faster. All he succeeded in doing was severing a vein. A scarlet plume spurted over the paper causing the guard to grunt and attempt to wipe it clean with a fat fist.

His companion lurched towards me. He ripped a strip of fabric from my petticoat and applied a rough bandage to the prisoner's wrist. The prisoner tried to resist, but the guard pinned his arm down and rammed the quill into his hand once more. When he'd finished writing, he collapsed across the desk. Guy Fawkes had just signed his confession.

Both guards then looked at me. Once again it was the largest who took the lead. He pulled a white-hot iron out of the brazier and limped purposefully towards me. I tried to crawl away but the chain jerked me back, cutting into my ankle. As the vomit started to rise in my throat, he told me that he was going to brand my cheek to make it clear that I belonged to the King. The heat of the iron and the stink of his rotting teeth grew stronger with every step he took.

For a second or so, I didn't register the vibrating and ringing of my mobile on my bra, but it had the effect of star-tling the guard who could see its light through the thin linen. He dropped the branding iron and I quickly rummaged and grabbed my phone. There was a missed call from Kenny, but also a text telling me they had a fix on my position and were bringing me home.

With an explosion of light, the chamber walls raced and stretched into infinity like a hall of mirrors. In a wink, I was tumbling through space and time. In a second, I appeared on a canal towpath, scaring the shit out of a cyclist who swore at me. A woman in her fifties, dressed in a Barbour with Hunter wellies and pulling a reluctant cocker spaniel, approached me, but then thought better of it and walked on. I steadied myself against an iron railing, drinking in the reek of green stagnant water, the scent of meadow flowers and diesel fumes from the main road. Then I threw up and passed out.

When I came to, I was in a hospital bed. Kenny and Tim were sitting next to me. Kenny was eating grapes and Tim was just looking worried. Tim pushed the bridge of his glasses, which he always did when he was anxious and handed me a cup of luke-warm tea.

'Ruthie! What happened?'

'You got me to the cellar in the House of Commons, boys, but an hour late! I didn't have a chance to interview Fawkes as he was setting up the gunpowder barrels. I got there a minute before the yeomen and I was arrested and tortured with him. I nearly died but don't worry!'

Tim looked concerned and rubbed his chin. Kenny wasn't worried. He was still eating grapes. I noticed my filthy 'period frock' slung over the back of a chair with the Selfridge's discount label still visible.

'Sorry Ruth, but I bet you got a great story. Throw in a few pictures and we could be talking Pulitzer.'

'Piss off!'

Five days later I was in my flat sitting on my new leather sofa with my laptop on my knees. I was going through the company accounts, an experience only made bearable by a bottle of Pinot, twenty Marlboro Reds and an eight pack of Ibuprofen. The bruising on my jaw was a fetching shade of violet, the gash having been sealed with a butterfly stitch, and it really hurt. I looked at the spreadsheet despondently, "Time and Space Year Ending 2020" had an ominous ring to it. Tim and Kenny had always hated the name of the firm. They both thought 'Time and Space' sounded like the name of a leisure magazine with lots of pictures of golden retrievers, stately homes and women in floaty frocks, not a news agency, but I put in most of the cash so that was that.

Making money wasn't a problem for us as chrono journalists or 'krojos' as we were commonly referred to. Loads of media organisations were getting into time travel but it didn't take us long to work out what mattered. People didn't want to know about Alexander the Great's campaign against the Persians or his journey to the Indus. They wanted to know how many women he'd slept with, what he looked like in a 'mankini' and what he thought about the latest Kanye West album. The important stuff.

Even though we had no financial worries, I still had to justify a three hundred grand time machine upgrade to my accountant in a meeting the following week. I could already see her chewing her pen and laughing maniacally. I took a gulp of red and reasoned that I could highlight our successes. The 'Out and About' feature with Ghengis Khan and the 'Sex and Shopping with Marie Antoinette' website had been massive. I was just wondering if I could classify buying a thirteenth century Bohemian lute at source as a tax-deductible expense – it was a competition prize after all. I was thinking that she'd probably go for it when the late night cosiness was shattered. My mobile vibrated with such ferocity it almost took the ashtray and my glass of Pinot off the coffee table. It was a text from Kenny. "ARE YOU IN?" Clearly, I was but it had turned eleven and I really wasn't in the mood for talking about boosting electromagnetic fields with mercury coils or 1980s Swedish death metal bands. I cleared away what was left of the wine and shoved my laptop in a drawer along with several spreadsheets stained green by high-lighter pen and headed to bed.

It was 3 a.m. and the sodium wash from the lone street light outside my flat flooded in uninvited. Too much wine meant that I had been unable to close the blinds. Had I heard it or was it just the noise of a bad dream? Then I definitely heard it. Three sharp staccato raps as though the knocker were trying to summon the dead. Who would come calling at this hour? Tim and Kenny possibly but three o'clock was pushing it, even by their standards. I hastily pulled on my kimono and stepped into my slippers. I shuffled through the lounge, inexplicably tidying up throws and cushions as I went. I looked through my peephole. Nobody. I opened the door and stepped out on to the carpeted landing, lit elegantly and uselessly by an upright standard lamp overlooking a dying, potted jojoba plant. Still nobody. I turned and there he was standing in my lounge.

'Jesus Christ!'

'Nah Ruth! 'Tis I, Guy!' he muttered without even a trace of a smile.

'Guy Fawkes! How can I help?'

Awful, I know, but it was the first thing that came into my head, even though I sounded like the Loan Officer of a High Street bank.

'You look a lot better than you did four hundred and twelve years ago.'

He told me that the pleasure was all his and bowed. In my shell-shocked state, however, I did notice that he'd clearly been shoplifting in Marks and Spencers. He was in a charcoal pin-stripe three-piece with a marigold tie and sporting novelty cufflinks. He could have been heading to work in the Crown Court but the footwear was less barristerial. Tan, embroidered cowboy boots with steel toecaps. Where he'd nicked those from, God only knows.

'Ruth! I need to hold counsel with you pertaining to an issue of the utmost urgency and consequence.'

It was going to be a long night. Whilst I was taking this in, he turned his head and there it was. A ponytail. How disappointing! The beard had also been replaced by sandpaper stubble. He now looked less of a seventeenth century terrorist and more like a pompous advertising exec. In short, a prat.

'How did you find me?'

'The fates have carried me to you on the wings of a divine wind. I also used the Google and the LinkedIn.'

Already, he was annoying. Indiscriminate use of the definite article made me think that actually hanging, drawing and quartering him was quite reasonable after all. Then from his jacket pocket he produced a gun.

"Tis with deep regret, Ruth, that I'm going to have to kill you since you are familiar with my countenance. May God have mercy on your soul!'

He aimed and then started stroking the top of the barrel as though trying to ignite an invisible flintlock. His bewilderment was palpable. He then started thumping it and swearing. I rushed at him but he was too quick and he struck me across the jaw, tearing open the stitch. I fell to the floor and noticed one of my shoes an arm's length away. I grabbed it and drove a stiletto heel into his kneecap. He buckled. Taking advantage of his pain and confusion, I picked up my weapon of choice and stabbed him in the arm. He limped out of my flat with my corkscrew hanging from his elbow, cursing me as 'a vixen she-bitch from the bowels of Hell and spawn of Medusa herself'. You know what though? I've been called worse by a sub-editor in Wolverhampton.

I looked out of my window and noticed a Vauxhall Astra bumping and kangarooing out of the car park. His lack of expertise with the horseless carriage gave me enough time to scribble down the reg.

Soon, there was a hammering at my door. It was Tim and Kenny. Tim looked like he was about to have a stroke. Kenny just looked as though he'd slept in a public toilet. Tim got down to business.

'Look, Ruth. Kenny and I have been going over the telemetry from your last jump home. We don't think you came back alone.'

'No shit!' I snapped, lighting another cigarette. 'You've just missed Guy Fawkes.'

Kenny had produced an apple and was wiping it on the sleeve of his Megadeath sweatshirt. For a second or two he looked disappointed that he'd missed him, but then he apologised for not coming round sooner. Tim just hugged me and his glasses steamed up. However, I had a question or two concerning our three hundred grand upgrade.

'Anyhow,' I continued, 'doesn't this new genetic locking system mean that that shouldn't happen?'

'He'd obviously picked up your DNA,' Kenny spluttered mid-bite. Tim, anxious as ever, took off his glasses and wiped them carefully. My brow must have furrowed as I remembered the guard using my frock as a tourniquet.

'You look worried, Ruth?' Tim said in a half-whisper.

'Well, Guy Fawkes is a highly trained mercenary, skilled at espionage, fluent in three languages and, quite frankly, also a homicidal nutter who wants to blow up Parliament, and we've given him a second chance. No, Tim. Everything's fine!'

Before too long, Mike, a police contact of mine, was sitting at my kitchen table nursing a beer. We only started making progress once I'd gone beyond, "Bloody hell, Ruth! I'll just add Guy Fawkes to my list of people to find after Joan of Arc and the Tooth Fairy". He was also going to talk to Interpol. To be fair on the coppers, they were slowly getting up to speed with the whole time travel thing. It was still in its teething stages, a bit like air travel in the thirties.

Mike's visit ended on a slightly dubious note when he stated confidently that Fawkes would be quite easy to find as he'd probably be wearing tights and not many men do. I wished him a good night and pretty much kicked Tim and Kenny down the stairs.

A fortnight later I was having a shower when my mobile rang. It was Mike. Guy Fawkes had been caught on his way to Brussels to blow up the European Parliament. Apparently, he was stopped at a service station just outside Bruges with a boot full of chocolate and plastic explosives. Kenny was able to get a lock on him and send him back to 1605, but not before I interviewed him and found out his fave top five cities in Europe and who he'd most like to be stuck in a lift with. Pope Gregory XII in case you're wondering.

My hair drier had been whining like a small marsupial and thinking hadn't been easy. I switched it off and stood in my kitchen towelling my wet hair. For the first time in about three weeks I felt relaxed. I breathed a sigh of relief and looked forward to the moment when some future archaeologist would find a Pierre Cardin tie pin and a pair of Kermit the Frog cufflinks in a seventeenth century unmarked grave.

Plump

Onize Osho

PLUMP: (full and round in shape).

It has reached the time of the month again,
Roundness creeps in, trifles begin to wane.
Come the steady waxing of the full moon,
My body ripens, in time to attune.
Look at the joyful spring in my footsteps,
Sturdiness in my thighs, legs and in – steps!
My sashay questioned, but the answers ride –
In rhythms borne from my ample backside,
And in my cosy, satisfied settle.
See, the dips and curves of my belly 'til
The roundness of my proportion'd waist.
I welcome now: the fullness of my breasts;
Curved shoulders leading to a solid neck;
Soft pointed chin (firm and strong when I check);
Lips – cinnamon and mocha, luscious red;
The shine in my dimpled cheeks and forehead;
The glow in my eyes and milky-white smile;
And glossy hair, so versatile in style.
This vigorous cascade of red, embrace
As we women do bear the human race.
Onwards! Empowered by Aphrodite,
Embrace our nature, might and beauty.

Shuttlecock

Salma Chowdhury

FADE IN:

INT. JAMIL'S BEDROOM - MIDNIGHT

INAYA (24, delicately pretty) enters wearing a red diamante dress. The bed is decorated with red rose petals, initials 'I' and 'J' are centred.

A phone hits the bed with a picture of two men kissing.

Rose petals scatter.

Inaya sits on the bed and screams.

JAMIL (30, petite and distinguished) runs in and closes the door behind him. His collar is unbuttoned and shirt is untucked. He throws his blazer on the bed.

Inaya wails loudly.

> JAMIL
> Shh, someone will hear you.

Inaya throws a pillow at Jamil. Jamil defends himself.

> INAYA
> What the hell was that, Jamil?!
>
> What do you expect from me?!

> JAMIL
> Look, I didn't think you'd see us.

> INAYA
> On my wedding night?! The night
> I've been waiting for!

>   (Throws another pillow)
>   What will my parents think?

Jamil kicks the pillows to the side.

>   INAYA (CONT'D)
>   We've been talking for 3 months
>   and you didn't think to tell me?!

Inaya viciously throws her bouquet of roses at
him.

>   JAMIL
>   Will you stop it?!
>   I'm sorry!
>   I had to do this!

He sighs, take his shirt off and throws it to the
bed. Then takes out panda print pyjamas from his
wardrobe.

>   INAYA
>   What do you mean you had to do
>   this?! Forced marriages are
>   haraam, remember?! You're clearly
>   not interested in me... or any
>   other woman.

>   JAMIL
>   My whole life is haraam!

Beat.

Inaya storms to the mirror and takes her earrings
off furiously. Jamil ignores her and puts his
bottoms on.

>   INAYA
>   So, why get married?

>   JAMIL
>   I'm 30 years old, my parents have
>   been begging me to get married for
>   10 years now. It'll look bad if I
>   didn't settle down with a woman.

                    INAYA
          That's your own issue, Jamil, why
          put me in this mess?

                    JAMIL
          I got so many proposals and you
          were the only one I liked... I
          thought we could be friends?

                    INAYA
          Wow, friend-zoned on my first
          night. Great.

Inaya takes a gold bangle off and throws it onto
the bed.

                    JAMIL
          I've known that I feel this way,
          since I was in my teens, but I
          tried to ignore the feeling.

                    INAYA
          You should have stuck to those
          feelings and left me alone.

                    JAMIL
          I'm sorry, I thought I could get
          over this... I've heard of men
          like me getting married and moving
          on.

                    INAYA
          You can't move on just like that.
          You proved that tonight.

She throws his phone at him.

                    JAMIL
          Inaya, please. Could we live
          together for a couple of months?
          You can do whatever you like.
          Then, we could get a divorce and
          I'll act heartbroken. I won't need
          to get married again. What do you
          think?

                    INAYA
       Divorce?!

Inaya rips off the roses stuck to the mirror.

                    INAYA (CONT'D)
       Allah blessed our marriage and you
       want to make a mockery out of it?
       Wow, you really are something
       special, Jamil.

                    JAMIL
       What do we do then? Neither of us
       will be happy like this.

                    INAYA
       I'm not giving up my life for this
       game you've made.

                    JAMIL
       It'll only be for a while, Inaya,
       then I'll be out of your life.
       Please, I have no other option.

Beat.

                    INAYA
       If that's the case, I'll be living
       my life how I like, for the next
       three months.

                    JAMIL
       Yeah? Whatever you want.

Beat.

                    INAYA
       I've always wanted to play
       badminton.

                    JAMIL
       Yeah, yeah, badminton's fine.

                    INAYA
       But my parents have always had an
       issue with the uniform.

                    JAMIL
          What do you mean the uniform?

                    INAYA
          I wanna wear the short skirt...

                    JAMIL
                    (raises his eyebrow)
          In that hijaab?

Inaya throws a pillow at him.

                    JAMIL (CONT'D)
          I know you probably don't want to
          hear this but one time, I had a
          fling with...

                    INAYA
                    (raises her hand)
          You've got to be kidding me!

EXT. COMMUNITY CENTRE.

Inaya walks in, wearing a short skirt with knee
high socks and a tight-fitting vest top. She pulls
her skirt slightly lower.

Her coach DAMIAN (26, mysteriously charismatic) is
applying sunscreen to his abs. Their eyes meet.

INT. LIVING ROOM - MORNING

Jamil's parents are sat on either side of the
room, watching T.V.

                    DAD
          What is this bullshit? I have Sky
          at home, not this bullshit Virgin.

                    MUM
          Only because you think Virgin is
          too expensive.

Dad looks at her and kisses his teeth.

                    MUM (CONT'D)
          Excuse me? Why are you being rude
          to me?

                    DAD
          You're wasting my son's
          electricity.

                    MUM
          He's my son too.

                    DAD
          Do you pay for half of his bills?

                    MUM
                    (Cries)
          Did you breast-feed him?

                    DAD
                    (Rolls his eyes)
          Oh, here we go.

Jamil enters and changes the channel to Bangla
channel. The news flashes on.

                    JAMIL
          Something you'll both watch.

                    DAD
          Your mother's crazy.

Mum blows into her tissue and wipes her tears.

Inaya enters with two cups of tea.

                    MUM
          Such a good daughter-in-law.

                    DAD
          Did you heat the cup?

                    INAYA
          Yes.

                    DAD
          Did you add half a spoon of honey?

                    INAYA
          Yes.

                    DAD
          Did you add one spoon of Horlicks?

                    INAYA Yes.
          He sips the tea and gives it back
          to her.

                    DAD
          You only put one sweetener in, I
          have two. Go make it again.

Inaya smiles awkwardly and looks up at Jamil.

                    JAMIL
                    (Takes the cup from Inaya)
          I'll make it, Dad.

                    MUM
          That is so sweet of you!

                    DAD
          Yes, that's it, do all the house
          chores like a real man.

                    INAYA
                    (awkwardly laughs)
          So how long are you staying for,
          Dad?

                    DAD
          Do you want us to leave already?

                    INAYA
          Oh no, just wanted to know so that
          I could take a few days off from
          work.

                    MUM
          Told you, she's a good daughter-
          in-law. We'll stay as long as you
          want us to.

Jamil enters. Inaya clears her throat and picks up a gym bag.

Dad spots the gym bag in the mirror.

> JAMIL
> Oh Mum, Dad, Inaya's going to be late for work.

> MOTHER
> Okay, shona, you go and have a good day.

> INAYA
> Khuda hafiz

> DAD
> Hmmm.

EXT. COMMUNITY CENTRE - DAY

Inaya is playing badminton with Damian.

Damian stops playing. He pants.

> INAYA
> (laughs)
> Am I getting too good for you, Damian?

Damian catches his breath. His eyes constantly follow her.

> DAMIAN
> Believe me, I've seen better.

Beat.

She stares back at him. He smiles. She smirks and throws a shuttlecock at him.

> DAMIAN (CONT'D)
> Oi!

He runs over to her and chases her to the bench with a towel.

They both sit down. Inaya drinks from her water
bottle and Damian watches her, intrigued.

Inaya catches him staring. Damian looks away.
She puts a stray strand of hair behind her ear -
she looks down at his body. He watches her. He
scratches his stomach, revealing his abs.

She stares.

> DAMIAN (CONT'D)
> (clears his throat, smiling)
> So, how are the in-laws?

> INAYA
> (sighs)
> It's been 3 weeks since they've
> come and it feels like forever.

She slouches down on a bench in front of him.

Damian starts to massage her shoulders.

> INAYA (CONT'D)
> (Flinches)
> You don't need to do that.

> DAMIAN
> You need to be less stressed if
> you wanna compete soon.

Inaya stands up and looks him in the eye.

Beat.

She puts her racket away.

> INAYA
> Do you wanna go for a coffee?

> DAMIAN
> We always go for a coffee. What
> about somewhere private?

> INAYA
> Well, I'm kind of swamped with my
> in-laws...

Damian begins to pack his kit away. His phone
rings, he answers it. Inaya checks her phone to
see 10 missed calls. Jamil rings.

> JAMIL
> Why is your phone always on
> silent?

> INAYA
> (to Damian)
> I gotta go, Damian, I'll see you
> tomorrow.

> DAMIAN
> Wait. What? Already?!

Inaya starts to run.

> INAYA
> It's urgent, I'll text you!

Damian rolls his eyes and carries on with his
phone call.

INT. JAMIL'S BEDROOM - EVENING

Jamil and Inaya sit on the bed, watching a film on
Netflix with a bowl of popcorn.

> JAMIL
> So what do you think he means by
> 'somewhere private'?

> INAYA
> I don't know. This feels so wrong.

Beat.

> JAMIL
> So what you gonna do?

Inaya fiddles with the tassels on her hijaab and
shrugs her shoulders.

> JAMIL (CONT'D)
> Just ask him to come over.

Mum knocks on the door.

                    JAMIL (CONT'D)
          Mum, we're busy!

Jamil starts to jump on the bed.

                    INAYA
          How long do we have to keep this
          up for? You're bouncing too hard.

They giggle quietly.

                    INAYA (CONT'D)
          It just doesn't feel right,
          Jamil... we're still islamically
          married.

Jamil's phone beeps and he gets it out of his bag.
A leaflet falls out.

                    JAMIL
          Hey, there's a new buffet around
          the corner.

                    INAYA
          Let's go!

                    JAMIL
          I have a better idea, let me take
          Mum and Dad, and you call him
          over!

Inaya is silent. She takes a huge handful of
popcorn and shoves it in her mouth. Jamil takes
the bowl away from her.

                    JAMIL (CONT'D)
          Stop being a chicken! Our marriage
          isn't even valid!

                    INAYA
          Technically, it is.

                    JAMIL
          Bit late with the technicalities.

>   INAYA
> OK, fine! Do we have to do it
> tonight?

>   JAMIL
> Yes! Text him right now!

Inaya twists her hijaab tassels and picks her phone up.

INT. LIVING ROOM - EVENING

>   MUM
> Are you sure you're going to be
> alright on your own?

>   INAYA
> Yes, mother, I need to get this
> paper work done.

>   JAMIL
> Alright, ring us if you need
> anything.

Dad walks out. Mum just looks at Inaya, Jamil pushes her out.

INT. LIVING ROOM - EVENING

Inaya sets the table with two plates and cutlery. She lights a candle. Door bell rings.

Inaya opens the door and Damian is waiting with gift box in hand.

She opens the box to find a shuttlecock with her name engraved. Inaya looks him in the eye and smiles.

She brings Damian in by his arm and they both sit down on the sofa.

EXT. CAR - EVENING

Dad is driving slowly. Jamil keeps glancing at his phone.

                    JAMIL
          Thought you used to be a taxi
          driver, Dad.

                    DAD
          This BMW cost a lot of money to
          rent.

                    MUM
          I feel bad that she's home alone.

                    DAD
          Your daughter-in-law is fine.

INT. LIVING ROOM - EVENING

                    DAMIAN
          I hate that you're in this
          situation.

Damian holds her hand.

                    INAYA
          I know but what can I do?

                    DAMIAN
          Leave him.

Inaya lets go of his hand.

                    INAYA
          And go where? My family won't have
          me back.

Damian grabs her hand.

EXT. CAR - EVENING

DAD is driving in circles to find parking.

                    DAD
          Should have brought my disabled
          badge.

                    JAMIL
          No, it's fine, you'll find a space.

> DAD
> No, I'm turning around now, we're
> not far from home anyway. It's my
> petrol, not yours.

Jamil quickly texts Inaya.

INT. LIVING ROOM - EVENING

Inaya's phone vibrates on the table. She is
kissing Damian.

Inaya pulls back and stares into Damian's eyes.

> INAYA
> Leave him and go where?

> DAMIAN
> Leave him and come to me.

> INAYA
> But I can't tell anyone he's gay.
> I'll get the blame for
> everything...

Mum enters.

> MUM
> Who's gay?
> (Sees Inaya and Damian)
> Inaya?!

Jamil enters.

> MUM (CONT'D)
> (to Jamil)
> Is it you she's talking about?

> JAMIL
> Ohh, err. I can explain...

Jamil stares at Damian.

Dad enters.

> DAD
> (Sharply)
> Damian?! What are you doing here?

                    DAMIAN
Masood? Err, err Mr. Hussain, it's
been a while. Everyone misses you
at the centre.

                    MUM
                    (To Dad)
It was him?!

                    Beat.
                    JAMIL
                    (looks at Dad)
Dad?
                    (looks at Damian)
Damian?!

                    DAMIAN
Jamil?

                    JAMIL
Oh my God, Damian?

                    INAYA
                    (looks at them both)
You've got to be kidding me!

                                        FADE OUT

Rabbit Show

Ali AElsey

Malcolm was famous at the Regional Rabbit Show for two things: his delicious 'bunny-buns' (mini rabbit shaped carrot cakes) and his champion rabbit, Charlie-Farley – a dwarf-lop with perfect coloration. Like his owner, Charlie had large hazel eyes, was always immaculately turned out and full of charm. During the setup that morning he'd been visited by many adoring regulars, who said he looked sensational and that the 'bunny-buns' tasted better than ever.

The show was definitely at maximum capacity this year, Malcolm noted, as he groomed Charlie before the first heat, with a blush-pink brush from his expensive rabbit manicure kit. Malcolm hummed confidently as he worked on the finishing touches to Charlie's coat. He knew the first judge was a fan of Charlie's.

Twenty exhilarating minutes later another Best-In-Class certificate was carefully added to Charlie's already bulging fuchsia-velvet folder. Malcolm, with toothy-grinned satisfaction, whispered, as he placed Charlie in his luxury portable-hut for a rest:

'We'll need Volume 2 soon, my lovely. Hope we can get one to match.'

Charlie calmly munched through a carefully-balanced Lapin-Peak™ power-lunch, while Malcolm had a cheap, supermarket tomato and cheese sandwich. Then Charlie 'did his business' prior to the next round. He never 'embarrassed' Malcolm like other rabbits did their owners.

By 3pm that year's Best-in-Breed certificate was also nestling in the folder and the marquee was filling up for the final event: Best-in-Show. There was only one thing troubling Malcolm at that point. How could he extend Charlie's prize shelf to accommodate another Winner's Plate? But then it happened. The tannoy announced that due to unforeseen circumstances the usual Final Judge; Mrs Caruthers, Chairwoman of the English Rabbit Appreciation League (R.A.L), a woman who adored Charlie, was being replaced by someone Malcolm and the breeders nearby had never heard of. A buzz ran through the competitors of speculation and panic as everyone set to work making certain their rabbits were in tip-top condition.

When the new judge, Miss Whipstrill, announced as Chairperson of the Welsh R.A.L; stalked into the ring, minutes later, Malcolm instantly remembered her as the gaunt, short-haired young woman who'd rudely refused to even taste a bunny-bun that morning because they weren't certified vegan! She hadn't even glanced at Charlie then and seemed to spend less time with him now than other contestants. She passed briskly along the line of rabbits performing the mandatory checks with barely a smile to any of the owners. Then, after a tense few minutes, awarded Best-in-Show to a complete novice; a rabbit nonentity, many suspected of having bleached hair, called Puffle Maximus Fluffius!

Malcolm seethed as the arena erupted with applause. The public obviously had no idea about true breeding. In truth, he hadn't much liked Mrs Carruthers, with her mane of red hair piled up under hats like gardens, massive bosom and bingo wings, but she had loved Charlie! Where was the silly woman? Malcolm fumed as he started to pack away Charlie's things, even wastefully binning the remaining 'bunny-buns'. No photos or interviews for them this time, all that was happening paces away, as the winning owner playfully placed his grotesquely pampered animal on the Winners Plate itself, for the Rabbit Times cover photo-shot! Everyone was crowded round him, no doubt anxious to be included in the public celebrations. Not one former Charlie-fan came to commiserate with him. Malcolm was upset to think how such rejection might hurt the rabbit's feelings.

Then a snatch of conversation drifted onto his ears, from two passers-by.

'Mr Caruthers is frantic,' said one woman to the other, as she paused to re-arrange her bags. 'Mrs Caruthers had only just got back from extensive makeover surgery that had cost him thousands. Breast reduction, lipo-suction – they'd even dyed that hair of hers, added extensions and given her blue contacts.'

'What a generous gift! I heard they were in the middle of their anniversary meal. She went to smoke one of those revolting menthol cigarettes she loves and vanished – wearing his dead mother's fur coat and diamonds! He was more bothered about losing them, according to Audrey Carter.'

The women laughed ghoulishly and walked on.

Malcolm stared after them for a moment, frowning, then started to pack faster than before. Even Charlie noticed the rapid swaying of his hutch, when minutes later they exited, without saying their usual goodbyes. Definitely a case of sour grapes, some thought, as Malcolm's pink Jaguar uncharacteristically sped out of the car-park.

Once home, Malcolm dumped Charlie unceremoniously with the bags in the hall, still in his portable hutch. He snatched a large key from its hiding place, under the wooden rabbit doorstop, flung open the door to the cellar and scuttled down the steps, as fast as his tight red Chinos would allow. He headed towards a large, chest-freezer humming against the back wall, behind the wine racks. Donning purple non-Latex gloves, he opened its huge lid, selected one of the turkey-sized bags and placed it carefully on his thick, wooden preparation table. Then he switched on small table lamp, unzipped the bag numbered 13 and examined the contents.

Malcolm groaned. It was his own stupid fault that his beloved Charlie had lost! Those startled blue eyes had been contact-lenses and the hair cropped and dyed, the body cut away – but it was her, Mrs Caruthers, he could see that now. So it was diamonds that had shattered the mincer-blades. No wonder she'd mumbled angrily through the gag, instead of looking scared, to start with. She would have recognised him. But why had she, of all people, agreed to wear a rabbit fur coat? He shivered with disgust. He'd buried it respectfully with the other twelve, in his back-garden memorial grotto, as his mother would have wished, surrounded by beautiful flowering bushes, which had the best fertiliser in the neighbourhood. The heads of the rabbit murder-ers couldn't go through the mincer, so he'd bagged and frozen them. In all these years Malcolm had never let a rabbit down. He stared at Mrs Caruthers for a moment, then started to cry for poor Charlie, who had already given up scratching at his hutch door upstairs and was now sleeping peacefully, dreaming of running free, in sunlit fields.

Post-Op

Alex Woodhouse

64 tiles in the waiting room, 173 here.

A far screech of wheels, one jug of water on his table, one cup on my table, no water, he's drinking tea. The bins to my right, one orange, biohazard symbol, one black, fire. Two bings.

Blood pressure taken, tightness leaves mark across muscle.

B.P. 154. 'Nervous?' 'No.' Don't know but 'No.' Suffice.

'He's cancelled, you can have the day off.'

Phone rings… 10 seconds, 30 seconds, One min. Picked up.

'I've been waiting 16 hours.'

I've been waiting 7 months. 2 years if you count the 'It's nothing, it's fine' routine.

'Can I take ma tablet now?'

'Yes, darling.'

Screwed up paper, next to it, biscuits. 20 minutes until tea and biscuits.

'It's gone a bit warm in here.' – 'Yeah.'

'It's boiling.' – 'To spread the disease.'

A laugh makes the mouth dryer.

She walks in with a jug of water.

'Got a cup?' – 'Yeah.'

One half a cup she fills. Not enough.

Full cup. Not enough.

Another half cup. Enough.

Another two bings coupled with vibration.

'Wife wanted BUPA, family package. No one can afford that.'

He sorts out sling for comfort.

One more cup. Too much.

Downed, head back, hold lips, get it down. Done.

'Do you want a cup of tea?' – 'Yeah' – 'Yeah, how many sugars?' – Bing.

'I've got bad circulation in my fingers'

'Usually find that with a diabetic.'

'I'm a diabetic.'

Rustle of paper. Rip of paper.

'Plenty of gloves.' Bing. 'Nice warm socks.'

Lunge forward. 'Hold on, I'll help you.'

'Bathroom first or get dressed?' – 'Dressed.' – 'Give us a shout if you...'

Tea's here, no biscuits.

'Sandwiches start in a bit.'

Screech of wheels. No. Nurse singing.

Tea is too hot for now, haven't eaten or drunk in 18 hours. First drop scalds.

'Got a nativity play tonight, the kids.' – Bing.

'Your break is now.' – Jovial 'Wahoo,' shouts the nurse.

'Can I get a cup of tea as well? two sweeteners,' he asks her.

Curtains rolled back. Fully dressed. Cast on.

'That'll keep you off work.' – 'Busiest time of the year.'

'Which one's the men's...left or right?'

'It's the left. They've changed it again. Went to the toilet, saw wet all over the seat. No woman's done that.'

'Sandwich or biscuits?' – 'Biscuits.' – 'Plain, custard, or bourbon?' – 'I'll have that one.' Bourbon was selected. First food in 18 hours. Tasted ok.

'...Don't bother to take me hum. – Fust time I've ever been in hospital, fust time I've ever been in hospital ... 80.'

Sleeping man wheeled in.

'Is he in the right ward? Is he in the right ward John?'

'Yeah he's in the right ward... just, not the right room'.

Sleeping man wheeled out.

Bourbons finished. Not eaten in 18 hours. Pacing is key.

Bourbons, possibly a sandwich, then maybe a full meal? Work my way up to the hog roast.

'Can you go now?' – 'Yeah, yeah.' – 'My son will come, he's shopping now.'

Two cups of tea brought in. One mine, one his. Given a dark red cup, can't remember if that was the previous cup. Should've taken a note.

'You can't leave now, you've had a general anaesthethic, you need 24 hours. I...'

Wheels screech, women wheeled past.

11:12 – Discussion of holidays taken.

11:19 – Discussion of holidays taken.

'Went to Magaluf, got robbed.'

'We got married in Vegas.'

Never took a holiday. Anaesthesia returning.

'On the night, it was freezing.'

Moving arms, heavy feeling.

'Sea of pink, it was amazing.'

Heavy feeling moves to head. Rest it on pillow.

Laughter, origin unknown. 6 tiles in view, 4 tiles, 1 tile. 2 Bings. 3 Bings. 6 Bings. Starts to sound rhythmic. Zero tiles. Zero Bings. Forty winks.

A Butterfly for Solomon

Esther Withey

FADE IN:

EXT. GARDEN- NIGHT

A moonlit garden. Silent. Empty. Except...

A BUTTERFLY lands on a leaf, pauses, and then flies away.

In its stead... An EGG.

INT. ATTIC BEDROOM - DAY

BETHAN (20) sits hunched over a desk, light from the window streaming onto the paper she's working on...

She's DRAWING. Rough sketches cover the paper, they're being shaded, scribbled over, erased. Exasperated, Bethan screws it up and aims for the bin.

MISSES.

She glares at the heap of discarded paper balls, sighs, and produces a fresh sheet.

INT. CARE HOME ROOM - DAY

A nursing home apartment, pristine but soulless.

Bethan displays her finished artwork to GLADYS, who, old and frail, looks panicked... She snatches the drawing, her eyes drinking it in.

                    GLADYS
          That's my Henry! How...

She DROPS it. Her face crumples and she begins to CRY!

JO, a middle-aged nurse, touches her arm,
reassuring.

>   JO
>   Miss Cookson's drawn him for you
>   Gladys. You remember showing her
>   your photos? And you've recognised
>   him!

>   GLADYS
>   But....He's so angry. Why did she
>   draw him so angry?

INT. STAFF ROOM — DAY

Jo stands with Bethan at a kitchenette.

>   JO
>   It wasn't that bad! You just made
>   him look a bit... harsh. Your
>   picture still helped her remember
>   and that's what we pay you for!

Bethan shrugs. She watches SOLOMON (6) crouched
on the floor, drawing the contents of a JAM JAR
resting on his knee.

>   BETHAN
>   I used to draw like that too.

>   JO
>   He was told to leave that at home.
>   He's supposed to be on homework!

Solomon looks up, indignant.

>   SOLOMON
>   This is work! It's an important
>   scientist project.

Jo rolls her eyes, but Bethan squats down beside
him.

>   BETHAN
>   I think that looks very important.

>   What's it for?

Solomon shyly shows her the NOTEBOOK he's been
drawing in.

Bethan flicks through a few pages, then reads
aloud...

                BETHAN (CONT'D)
      My Butterfly, By Sol. Is that you?

                SOLOMON
      Don't be silly! of course it is.

He points to a picture on the next page.

                SOLOMON (CONT'D)
      I found him in the garden. He's
      going to get bigger and bigger,
      and I'm going to record it as he
      grows into a butterfly.

                BETHAN
      I love butterflies too! Will you
      show me your picture of him when
      he's all grown up?

Solomon glares at her.

                SOLOMON
      No! I'm going to set him free when
      he's a butterfly, not draw him. And
      I'm going to be a scientist, so
      you have to call them diagrams,
      not silly pictures! You're mean!

Jo starts at this, turns Solomon to face her.

                JO
      Less of that lip young man.

She glances down at the book.

                JO (CONT'D)
      And while I'm at it, I've told you
      not to call yourself Sol. You've
      got a lovely name, and if you
      can't write it in full then I'll

> think you can't spell it!

>   SOLOMON
> I can too spell. Just not a stupid
> old man's name!

Bethan straightens up. She's suddenly nervous,
fidgeting.

>   BETHAN
> It's my Dad's name.

>   SOLOMON
> I bet he hates it!

>   BETHAN
> I don't know. He died before I was
> born.

>   SOLOMON
> He died?

>   JO
> Mmm, I remember your mum telling
> me when you first applied here.

>   BETHAN
> I guess she didn't want people
> to make a fuss. She can't even
> bear to have any pictures of him
> because they'd make her cry..
> But I still imagine him...

Bethan IMAGINES--

A young man strolls in, tall and tanned, on his
finger is perched... a BUTTERFLY!

>   BETHAN (CONT'D)
> I always picture him differently.
> He's whatever I need him to be.

EXT. GARDEN- DAWN

Deep in the undergrowth, a small movement. The egg
HATCHES.

INT. KITCHEN- DAY

A cluttered room. MANDY is elbows deep in washing up. She jumps as Bethan enters.

> MANDY
> You're early.

Bethan shrugs, and heads towards the door.

Mandy hastily dries her hands, rushes to GRAB BETHAN'S ARM.

> MANDY (CONT'D)
> Hey! What's gone on? You were at
> St. Luke's today weren't you....
> did something happen?

> BETHAN
> I don't want to talk about it.

Mandy leads Bethan over to a chair.

Awkward silence.

> MANDY
> Please at least tell me you got
> paid.

Rolling her eyes, Bethan produces a handful of NOTES.

> BETHAN
> See. Apart from scaring an old
> lady and insulting a little boy
> it's good. Happy?

Mandy's head drops into her hands. She looks up, wearily.

> MANDY
> Will they have you back?

> BETHAN
> Yep. I'm drawing the boy a
> butterfly to make it up to him.

                    MANDY
          But he won't pay you?!

Bethan imagines-

Man enters, now blond and tubby, but still with a
BUTTERFLY perched on his finger. He stands behind
Bethan, takes her hand. Strengthened, Bethan looks
Mandy in the eye.

                    BETHAN
          Solomon.

Mandy jumps.

                    MANDY
          What?

                    BETHAN
          The boy's name.

Mandy looks away, pretending not to hear.

                    BETHAN (CONT'D)
          Dad's name! About the only thing I
          know about him.

                    MANDY
          Don't start.

                    BETHAN
          Why? He's been dead 20 years. You
          can't fob me off with 'too soon.'

INT. ATTIC BEDROOM- NIGHT

Bethan sits at her desk. She's sketching a man,
who now ginger, with butterfly on finger, is
lounging on the bed.

FOOTSTEPS echo upstairs! Panicked, Bethan hastily
covers her drawing with an equally detailed
BUTTERFLY SKETCH as... Mandy enters, holding an
ENVELOPE.

> MANDY
> Things er, got out of hand
> downstairs. I wanted to apologise.

> BETHAN
> It's fine. Forget it.

The man moves aside as Mandy perches on the edge
of the bed.

> MANDY
> No it's not love. I was thinking.

Haltingly, blinking fast, she passes the envelope
to Bethan.

> BETHAN
> What is it?

> MANDY
> Not much. But you should have it.

Bethan opens the envelope, pulls out a PHOTO...

Examines it. A young gawky man grins at the
camera.

Bethan places the photo carefully on her desk. She
compares it to her previous sketch, makes a couple
of changes. Mandy fidgets awkwardly. Reaches to pat
Bethan's shoulder.

Bethan recoils.

> BETHAN
> You do realise that's the first
> proper picture you've shown me.

> MANDY
> I know that. I'm sorry.

Bethan re-examines the photo.

> BETHAN
> 'Sol'?

>   MANDY
>   It's what he went by. 'Solomon's
>   an old man's name.' he said.

EXT. GARDEN- DAY

Wind blows through the garden, rustling the leaves
of a bush. Along one of them a caterpillar is
crawling... drops!

Falling?

No, attached to the underside, it begins to spin a
cocoon.

INT. LIVING ROOM - DAY

Mandy sits on the sofa, poring over a newspaper
cutting-

'LOCAL ARTIST IN TRAGIC CAR CRASH'

She touches her cheek, rubs away a tear.

Bethan appears in the doorway.

>   BETHAN
>   Mum?

Mandy jumps, stuffs the paper down the sofa
cushion.

Bethan sits next to her.

She glances at the doorway where the man from the
photo, IMAGINED SOL, has appeared! He gives her a
thumbs up.

>   BETHAN (CONT'D)
>   Mum? About Dad. I wanted to ask...

Mandy shoots Bethan a warning look.

>   BETHAN (CONT'D)
>   It's nothing bad, I promise.
>   But...
>   I want to go see him.

Mandy springs from the sofa. She looks alarmed.

> BETHAN (CONT'D)
> Please. I just want to want to
> go to his grave. Be a proper
> daughter. I just need to know
> where he's buried...

EXT. CEMETERY- DAY

A graveyard. Bethan wanders between tombstones,
her eyes scanning them as she passes. Imagined Sol
beside her, she reaches the cemetery gates.

Sighs.

> IMAGINED SOL
> You okay?

Bethan draws a hand across her face.

> BETHAN
> I don't get it. Mum said it was
> here!

> IMAGINED SOL
> No she didn't.

> BETHAN
> Not directly, but she said it was
> a rushed burial and this is the
> only cemetery for miles... she
> wouldn't have had time to put him
> anywhere else.

Bethan searches her bag, finds the NEWSPAPER
CLIPPING...

> BETHAN (CONT'D)
> I swiped it from mum before we
> left... she didn't notice.

> IMAGINED SOL
> What does it say?

> BETHAN
> I haven't read it yet... but it's
> dad's picture. I guess, maybe

it'll confirm if he's here or not.

She begins to read... turns white!

Over her shoulder, imagined Sol reads aloud...

> IMAGINED SOL
> It's thought that Solomon Cookson
> will never recover full cognitive
> ability... He's to be moved to
> St. Luke's Institution for the
> Mentally Handicapped-

Bethan stands perfectly still, dumbstruck.

> IMAGINED SOL (CONT'D)
> St Luke's? But... isn't that where
> you work?! How could you not know?

Bethan shakes her head. In a daze, she walks a few
steps...towards the nearest tombstone. She pulls a
pencil and sketchbook from her bag.

There's a BUTTERFLY, on the stone.

Hands shaking, she puts pencil to paper, and
DRAWS...

INT.LIVING ROOM - DAY

Mandy frantically paces the room. Hands balled
into fists she mutters words, phrases, only just
audible.

Bethan sits on the sofa, her face blank as she
listens.

> MANDY
> I stand by it, I do. Stupid man. I
> wish he really was dead! You don't
> know what he was like.

Bethan leans forward, imploring.

> BETHAN
> Then tell me, please. I just want
> the truth. From you.

>   MANDY
>   You want the truth? That's nothing
>   but arguments... drink... he left
>   us Bethan. I was just a few weeks
>   from giving birth and he left.

Mandy's broken. She hunches up into a ball and
cries.

Bethan wraps her arms round her, rocking,
soothing.

>   MANDY (CONT'D)
>   I couldn't stop him. He didn't
>   want to stay... just stormed
>   out... then the accident happened
>   and... when he woke up that nurse
>   you like so much.... she was the
>   one at his bedside... it should
>   have been me... she was the one
>   helping him, teaching him.... yes
>   he remembered her alright....
>   nobody else. nothing....
>   everything before her was gone...
>   the lie is easier. In the lie...
>   he LOVES US.

INT. CARE HOME CORRIDOR- DAY

An empty corridor, lined with doors. Bethan slopes
along, holding her SKETCHBOOK. Jo is bustling in
the opposite direction.

>   JO
>   Bethan! I wasn't expecting you.

Bethan smiles uneasily.

>   BETHAN
>   I, er, wanted to give this to
>   Solomon. For his project.

She holds out a page. It's the DRAWING from the
cemetery, tearstained and desperate but beautiful
in its sadness.

                      JO
For my Solomon? It's beautiful.

Bethan tries to talk, but falters, stares at the
ground.

                   JO (CONT'D)
What is it, pet?

                   BETHAN
I, er, look, do you know where a
Solomon Cookson is?

Jo's face changes from calm to panicked in an
instant.

                    JO
Your mum didn't want me to tell
you anything. When you took the
job... I had to make sure you
were never asked to draw for him,
he leaves his room so rarely the
chances of you two meeting were
pretty much zero... but he's come
so far since the accident...

Bethan nods, too choked up to speak.

                   JO (CONT'D)
I don't know what to say. Just…

She GESTURES TO A DOOR.

Bethan follows her gaze. She looks terrified.

Takes a few, tentative steps forward.

Imagined Sol stands behind her.

                  IMAGINED SOL
He won't be the same you know. As
me.

                   BETHAN
I know. But he will be him.

Bethan stands in front of it for a moment, hesitating.

She turns the handle.

EXT. GARDEN- DAY

The chrysalis starts to move as... A BUTTERFLY EMERGES.

                                        FADE OUT

How to Start Again
Lucy Farrington-Smith

In eleven days I will be twenty-four.

In four and three-quarter hours, it will be midnight, the sun falling from view in a dozy thirty. Five minutes and fifty-two seconds are left ticking by before my playlist switches track. There's one cup of cold coffee on my bedside table.

Today was the first.

It's been forty-one days of being inside, looking out. A *spectator*; not a participant. Somewhere in my twenty-three years and three hundred and fifty-four days, I lost my admission pass, dropped my ticket stub- I twisted up the receipt until it was just a balled mass of black on white.

Somewhere in those years, I gently, and all-at-once, let go of my mind.

And it's strange. It's strange how we are the puppeteers of our own thoughts, able to pull cords and tie knots in our own supplies of blood and air. How we have the ability to do *everything* and nothing, to live and breathe; to give up, and let go. It's strange how your own mind can play tricks on you. How it can become a separate entity, detached, and able to make you believe in the unnatural, the irrational; the inescapable.

And it's terrifying when you begin to realise how your mind can push you. To dread sleep for fear of not waking; yet dread being awake because *every second* is like the last, plagued with irrational fears conjured by your own Machiavellian creation.

Where food is poison. Sleep is impossible. Minutes seem infinite. Shaking is constant. You don't want to cry, and yet, at the same time, *all you want to do* is cry. Your eyes are open, but the nightmare doesn't stop.

But today was the first.

Forty-one days. Behind layers of glass and brick, letting my eyes live the life I want. Watching the raspy pull of branches billowing above the footsteps of neighbours. Trapped behind a window with envy for their life, their purpose; *their simple ability to leave their home*.

But today was different. Today, the windows didn't magnify the world. The glass didn't encase me like a snow globe's orb, rooting my body thickly in place in plastic and ceramic and dull glitter. This time I wasn't a motionless figure watching the outside dance in endless pirouettes, sixes and eights of tulle passing me by like the mist of affection in the arrivals lounge of an airport.

It's been forty-one days of the ordinary seeming impossible. Of rooms feeling smaller. Tastes being clumsy and mismatched. Days where love feels claustrophobic. Support feels like failure. Where life feels like a trap.

Forty-one days where someone else's mundane was my Everest.

I experience anxiety. I don't *suffer* from it - it's dripped into my chromosomes, melted into my blood and built up in the pigment of my eyes. I accept it as part of me.

Today was the first time in forty-one days I felt able to leave home on my own again. And it was strange. Like stepping onto ice, and learning how to swipe your feet. My shoes felt odd. My arms didn't know how to swing. I didn't know where to look, and the sun seemed brighter than it should. But I was outside, and I was alone. *Surviving*. Breathing. Overcoming fear.

In eleven days I will be twenty-four. And I'm still learning. How to live inside the body I have grown; how to shake someone's hand firmly enough, how not to cry in public and how to turn around on a busy pavement when you know you're walking the wrong way. I'm learning how to live with the thoughts that manifest in my head when something gets too much.

And if I have to accept that the next eleven, twenty, or fifty days are spent learning how to cope and start again, I will. *Our feelings are fluid; our experiences eternal*. Memories can be lost, but the muscle remains. I'm training myself to live in a world that is evolving faster than we can see.

Anxiety makes you believe the unbelievable. The *impossible*. The bang-your-head-against-the-wall stupid. But to you, it can seem as real as anything, as routine as a heartbeat. And if today I experienced my first steps again for a second time, I'll learn how to start again.

I'm not ready to give up before my new chapter has had a chance to begin.

The Pact

Gregory Leadbetter

A *secret place* was all the note said
of where to meet. I chose the woods I walked
the time I lost the key to my house,
returning to find a stranger asleep
on my bed, who woke to say sorry, he got tired
while waiting. Since then I've been writing,
letting the phone ring, dropping my friends.
The work grew like a child between
my daylight hours, a nine-month seal
of shared blood, melted in the wax
of a waning flame that tapered to a scrawl
I knew as mine, telling me *go tonight*.

The figure in liquid silhouette
stepped from the sky between a symmetry
of silver birch, quiet as the morning star.
Held in the split and dawn-red eyes
I felt the kiss of a voice on my throat
sing through my skin with the touch of the air.
I don't know how long I was weightless
in the promise of those words. They
thinned to silence as the sky paled.
I stretched in the darkened sun, mindful
of what would be waiting in my empty house,
whether it would return this greater loss.

Dipping

David Roberts

The Oateses of Norfolk: brewers and weavers, humble fabricators who saw God's word not in altars and communion cups but in the scent of flowers and tight-woven cloth upon the loom. But young Samuel Oates had long tired of making Norwich stuff. The day he saw an angel dance upon the wool he was drawing out with his right hand, he knew he must become a prophet, and he left for London.

It was not for the war's sake. When other Norwich men were leaving their barrels and their looms to drill for the regiments of Parliament or muster cock-hatted under the King's own standard, Samuel took off to join another army. He did not find it straight away. For days he wandered the streets of London, looking for the sign, until one day he chanced, blistered and hoarse, upon Bell Alley, off Coleman Street. The door was ajar and he heard the true voice of the Lord in the rough-hewn benches and lime-washed plaster. They welcomed him in, called him Brother.

'Seek, and ye shall find,' someone said.

'You must rest with us,' soothed another.

'Here is some water.'

'The Lord's pure water.'

'Drink, for you thirst.'

So he took the cup and his blood caught fire.

That night, they told him of their cause.

'We are children of God,' explained their leader, a man with a hedge beard and a wan eye, 'through King David. We answer to no magistrate; no human law binds us. We render the power of the sword only to ministers and prophets, and judge all cases by scripture. It is the only law.'

'And what of princes and worldly governors and parliament men?' Samuel asked.

'All such will be consumed in fire,' said the man, his face bright with hope. 'It is God's will. We live in common. If you do not share your goods, there is no salvation for you. If you do not render to us your wife and receive our wives in return, you may not be saved. If you covet learning and claim special knowledge of the scripture, you will be damned, for it is only the meanest and most humble of mankind that may speak for Christ. We speak only as the Holy Ghost tells us. We are moved by the Spirit so that all your princes and worldly governors and parliament men will be laid waste and Christ will reign eternal.'

Samuel did not have to wait long for the Holy Ghost to tell him to speak. The bare room in Bell Alley was called Lamb's Church, and he preached there with the rest of the brethren. He was warned against calling it a sermon, so he learned to think of his speeches instead as acts of witness. Sometimes the Holy Ghost led him to wonder how he could possibly have been so corruptingly sophisticated, as a mere weaver of Norwich worsted. How could he have believed that God had preordained designs for every man? Was it really unlawful for a man to sleep with a woman other than his wife? Or, sleep being a kind of death, why was it not permitted for a man to be with another woman while his wife was napping? And so the flame burned strong within him to speak Christ's word; and so, imagining those other women, he craved one for himself.

He got his wish in Hastings. The brethren had sent him into Sussex to bring light to the sinful abyss they discerned there. On the very fringes of Albion he found his Lucy. A midwife, she was known for a pious and virtuous sort. It was Samuel's proposal of a dipping that enticed her. The thrill of it: to be baptized at midnight, stealing out of her father's house, down to the river, naked at the hands of the prophet Samuel. It was said of him later that wherever he had been a-dipping and bringing fresh brides into the church, women who had been married for several years and never were with child suddenly found themselves pregnant. Truly, Samuel swore, it was the Lord's work. A few of their husbands rejoiced; others withheld their gratitude, plans of vengeance stirring.

When the war was over and the tyrant King imprisoned, Samuel passed on to Essex. He travelled the county disrupting church services, denouncing ministers and calling the local constabulary agents of the antichrist. Crowds followed him, some of them barren wives who yearned for a dipping. If the officers of the law turned out, he would rustle up a band of apprentices and call a riot. Alarmed by the upheaval, the Chelmsford magistrate could not resist the joke that had been going round, though he cracked it with gall in his throat: 'this fiery preacher, this self-appointed prophet, this revolutionary Anabaptist, has been all over the county sowing his tares, his boolimong, his *wild oats*,' he snarled. Hundreds of women, he cried, had been seduced; scores had been dipped in the Blackwater River at Bocking, then gorged on midnight feasts which Oates had the nerve to call the Lord's Supper. Yet it was no use sending him to prison, where he would only convert others to his cause. Another way must be found.

Samuel's cause may have been holy, but his rewards were worldly. Dipping came at a price. Poorer women he charged two shillings and sixpence; the richer sort, ten shillings. His dipping labours, observed a fellow traveller, were 'abundantly blessed' - more than could be said for the dipped. One night a woman screamed and screamed as she surfaced.

'Down with her again!' cried Samuel. 'It is the devil in her flesh. She must be made clean!'

So she was dipped again. Again she screamed, and again he

dipped her. At her fourth surfacing he saw the knot of brambles that had caught her foot, and the blood that flowed down river.

'It is a sign of God's favour,' he whispered in her ear as he pushed hard against her breasts.

Then one night in April, when a late winter gripped the Essex marshes, he ventured out to the river with a woman of twenty called Ann Martin. She had approached him after the Ghost had been truly upon his tongue and said with a smile flickering round her mouth that she was thirsting for salvation and the rule of Christ. Her eye was wild, he thought, and she was flushed at the neck. She coughed with a deep rattle. As they stood on the bank she pulled her shift up over her head and cast it into the water. He wondered at the miracle of God's work that made her full breasts stand so, and vowed to dip her as ardently as any maid he had ever baptized. But how unnaturally she shivered.

'Are you well, mistress?' he asked, not untenderly.

'I wish to be made well,' she said.

So he took her in his arms, his words on her cheek and his hand curling under her breast, and waded to the middle of the river. Even he was surprised by the cold, and caught his breath. When he lowered her into the water, she gave out a shriek such as he had heard from women in the height of passion. He brought her up. Already her hands were blue.

'You are received into the church of Christ,' he pronounced. But she would not have it.

'You must make me clean,' she urged. 'Again.' So he dipped her once more. But when he brought her out, her shuddering frightened him. Wrapping her in her shift, he carried her back to her mother's house, left her at the door, and ran.

The charge was murder. Ann had been found by her mother in the early hours and carried to her bed. She had lain sick and feverish for days. Delirious, she had kept crying out that she was a bride of Christ who had been brought into the church by the Baptist himself. They could send for the man and ask him if they did not believe her. But the coroner knew what to believe. Samuel was hunted down and thrown into Colchester jail.

Other charges, convenient for putting down rebellion, were laid against him. The constable visited him one day to list them, holding a nosegay before his face as, his hand trembling a little, he read out the list:

'You have preached against the laws of Parliament.'

'I have preached the law of Jesus,' smiled Samuel.

'You have ordered the people not to pay taxes.'

'Jesus collected no taxes.'

'You have incited disobedience.'

'We Saints are free people. Our will cannot be forced. We do what we do of our own accord and no man else's. It is the way of Jesus.'

When the constable left, a crowd was starting to gather outside the jail. A murmur started that it was a heinous sin indeed to imprison one of the Lord's true Saints. Stones were thrown and the militia called. As the crowd dispersed, a man was heard to say that there were many ways to ensure a Saint such as Samuel might be spared the rope.

He was right. Fathers and husbands across Essex wondered how it was that a jury could be stuffed with rascals of Samuel's own mind. Instead of being hanged, the Colchester Saint was bound over to good behaviour and ordered not to preach or dip within the county boundary. But Saints being free people and followers only of Jesus, Samuel merely made his way to Chelmsford and preached there the very next Sunday.

He found that Saints were not the only ones who could bypass the law. Aggrieved fathers and husbands, hearing of Ann Martin's sorry fate and wondering when it would come knocking at their doors, resolved to act. At Wethersfield a rumour went around that Samuel and his friends were on their way to the village. Men gathered with cudgels by a stand of elms and waylaid them early in the morning, with the mist cladding the meadows. For such meek and godly fellows Samuel's companions put up a stern fight; knives and axes were no strangers to the roving Saints, it seemed. Still, they were driven back bloody and bruised.

Their leader was not amongst them. He had gone alone to Dunmow, fierce in the pride of his mission and ready to dip a score or two of such maidens and matrons as were ready to see the light. The men of Dunmow were ready for him. From the tavern, from the baker's, from the blacksmith's and the basket weaver's, from the school and from farms for miles around they gathered. Their visitor was thought to have settled in a hovel just beyond the end of the high street. There they went, broke down the door, and carried him to the river. And in the river at Dunmow he had such a dipping as never maid or man endured. He was dipped to an inch of his life.

Later he would say that gossips, bawds and devil-worshippers had 'unfortunately impaired' his reputation in Essex. So he accepted counsel from the Lord and never went there again.

West Road, Cambridge

J Mann

7pm walks down the lamp lit roads, past
The cycles retired for the day,
Past the masses of colleges and the robed boys
Flowing out of their late Wednesday lecture.
We always went out mid-week,
One time we walked from Wednesday to the following Tuesday
Talking about how life is just one long day.
We sat our bums down on the wooden benches and waited for
    Prynne to arrive
He sat down and told us he forgot his handouts

He had forgotten his handouts

We had to listen attentively
You were bored, I could tell— I didn't have time to care
I had just made it to the talk of my lifetime I didn't want to
    come alone
- something funny - don't lecture me on the ethics of
    "inserting" humour
[Here's the bit I wrote the entire poem for]
For you and for what we heard that day
"The problem with food is that anyone can eat it"
We all laughed, we knew the truth deep down

See you next week

Caught in the In-Between
Danny Maguire

He waited for Death. He was already dead, but Death had yet to claim him from the wasteland in which his soul resided. He didn't know how long he'd been here, but he knew it was longer than he should have been. He remembered his life and his death – that most of all. He hadn't seen it coming but he remembered the feeling of the lance forcing its way through his ribcage and tearing a hole in his chest. He hadn't wanted to die, but Death had seemed to think that it was his time. At least that's what he'd thought.

To Eoghan, this new world had looked just like the battle-ground where he had died. When he first awoke, the colour had been drained out of the landscape; everything looked cold and grey. To him, it had seemed like a great fog had fallen on the land and absorbed almost all the colour and the life from it. His world was clearest on the spot where he died. As he moved away from it, fog grew denser until, when he was a certain distance away, the whole world disappeared, except for one small place. No matter how far he travelled, he could always see the area where he had died.

Then time changed the place. The green fields, beautiful trees and flowers which once covered the place had quickly vanished under strange stone structures. The ground, where his bare feet could once be tickled by the long blades of grass, was now rivers of a strange material, black as pitch, flowing around islands made of grey stone. He didn't understand how or why. As the field was destroyed, he recoiled at the idea of losing what he now called home, fearing he would lose all memory of the field where he had died in battle, and his memory of his life along with it. Once his panic had subsided, he discovered something.

It originally happened when he first began to relax. If he sat on the exact site of his death, closed his eyes and concentrated, he could return to the world he knew and the field he had grown to love. The buildings and roads disappeared and the green returned to him. However, this exhausted him. He wasn't sure how his soul got tired but it did, and only sleeping would reinvigorate him. Eoghan slept a lot.

The greatest thing about sleeping, was that he could bend his dreams to his will. When he first died and first dreamed, he dreamt of his family. He went home to his wife and two children. He kissed them, hugged them and laughed with them; but as with the living, every dream must end. He would wake up and feel low and full of sorrow for the rest of the day. He continued this, night after night, returning to his family, enjoying time with them, even if it was imagined. Day after day, he would wake up and have heartache envelope him until he went to sleep again. After years of swinging like a pendulum between love and loss, he could no longer stand it. He chose to dream of his family less and less, until he stopped dreaming of them altogether, but he never forgot them.

He saw no people in this world. At least, none living. When the field on which he had died was ploughed up, the grass simply rolled over by itself and buildings grew, without tools, without sound, without life. However, Eoghan caught glances of other souls; arriving in the distance, stumbling around in confusion for an hour or so, before being whisked away by a cloaked figure. It was strange that nobody seemed to die in the area in which his soul resided. Every soul he saw was far away from him, shrouded by the fog.

One day, Eoghan started to scream. Not in pain or madness, just boredom. He screamed, yelled, shouted, even sang for a long while. Until...

'Are you alright?'

Eoghan yelped, spinning around fast. He discovered another soul standing just a few feet away from him. It was the soul of a man, just like him, who seemed to be somewhere in his twenties, just as Eoghan had been when he died. The man had curly black hair, a white shirt and a strange pair of blue leggings.

'I'm-I'm fine,' Eoghan said, his voice an octave higher than usual.

'Then why were you screaming?'

'I was bored.'

'You scream when you're bored?'

'You would too, if you'd been here as long as I have.' A thrill shot through him. There was another person here. One he could talk to. It had been so long since he'd had a conversation. He ran to the new arrival, grinning like an idiot.

'Greetings, friend,' said Eoghan. The man stepped back, giving him a wary glance.

'Hello...' he said.

'Sorry,' Eoghan said quickly. 'It's been such a long time since I've spoken to anyone. At least, someone real. Not a dream person."

'Right...,' said the man.

'What's your name?'

'Caius.'

'I'm Eoghan.'

'Nice to meet you, Eoghan,' Caius said. 'I think.' Cautiously, Caius extended his hand. Eoghan eyed it, confused. 'It's a handshake. A gesture of peace.' Although unsure, Eoghan grasped the other man's hand and they shook.

'I'm sorry if I made you feel uncomfortable,' blathered Eoghan, excited to be speaking to someone at last, trying to cram as many words into his conversation as possible. 'I really am, but I've been alone here for a very long time. Centuries, I think, although I'm not exactly sure.'

'Where are we?' Caius asked, relaxing somewhat.

'I think it's the bit in-between death and the afterlife. This seems to be mine,' said Eoghan.

'Oh. Yeah, I've heard of this place. Purgatory, right? So, how did you die then?'

'I was a warrior, I died in battle. An enemy threw his lance across the battlefield and it went straight through my chest. Right here.' Eoghan lifted his baggy white tunic, revealing the wounds in his chest. 'How about you?'

'You were a soldier? Where's your armour?' said Caius. 'And your shoes?'

'Oh, armour is horribly uncomfortable. When I woke up here I took it off and put it over there.' Eoghan pointed vaguely. 'And I've always hated footwear. I love the feeling of the grass on my bare feet.' He smiled.

'There's no grass here,' said Caius, staring around. 'And your trousers are torn.'

'Of course, they're torn, I wore them into battle,' he said, looking down at his brown breeches. 'There was grass here once. Back when I died. I can change the landscape to how it used to be if I shut my eyes and concentrate. Tires me out, though.'

Caius raised an eyebrow. Shrugging, he sat down on the road, and Eoghan followed suit. 'My death wasn't anything noble like yours. I was hit by a car that was going stupidly fast. I died straight away. I supposed that's a blessing; it means I didn't have to suffer in pain.'

'That's a horrible way to die,' said Eoghan, sympathetically. He imagined being trampled by horses and a heavy wooden cart being much more painful than a spear through the chest. 'I mean, I knew death was probable when I went into battle, but you had no idea.' Then a realisation hit Eoghan hard. 'Oh, gods.

Death will be coming for you and will see me, so I can finally confront him for forgetting about me!'

Caius raised an eyebrow. 'I'm glad my death could be of service,' he said, dryly.

Eoghan wasn't sure if he was being serious, so he just smiled in a way that he hoped conveyed gratitude and apologies. After that they sat and talked for a while. They discussed their pasts and what their dreams once were for the future. Often, Caius lost his composure and would break down in tears.

In what seemed like no time at all, their wait was over. Death arrived, standing silent and hooded in the centre of the road. Eoghan and Caius, rose to their feet and faced him. Then, drawing close, the hood was lowered to reveal the face... the face of a young woman, framed with cropped blonde hair. She appeared to be around twenty years-old and perhaps the most beautiful woman Eoghan had ever seen. The woman was dressed in a black robe, which accentuated the colour of her hair.

'Hello, Caius,' she said. Her voice was perfect, sending a warm glow through Eoghan's soul. She smiled politely. 'Do you know who I am?'

'Death?' said Caius, a little unsure.

'Of a sort,' she said. 'My name is Niamh. I am the goddess of one of the Otherworlds. I've come to take you on to Tír na nÓg, or the Land of the Young in your language.' She held out her hand to Caius. 'If you would like to come with me.'

'Hold on,' said Caius. 'What about Eoghan?'

Eoghan cast Caius a grateful glance before looking back at Niamh. He tried to speak but his throat seemed to have closed up. Niamh gave Eoghan a distasteful look.

'Eoghan has been here for centuries. You've either completely ignored him or you've forgotten about him.'

'Eoghan is currently serving his punishment,' said Niamh, candidly.

Eoghan's heart fell to his stomach. *Punishment? What was he being punished for?*

'Purgatory is both a place of waiting and a temporary, light punishment.'

Light!

'If Eoghan had been sent to Hell, then it would be permanent. He would be suffering a terrible punishment for eternity. You should be thankful, Eoghan, that you are here and were not taken straight to Hell.'

'W-wait,' said Eoghan. 'Why am I being punished? I don't remember doing anything that deserves this punishment.'

'Perhaps that is why you are still here," said Niamh. 'Purgatory exists as a punishment for people to atone. To genuinely ask for forgiveness. Only then will they be free from this place.'

'But how am I supposed to atone for sins I can't remember committing?' Eoghan yelled.

'I'm afraid that is not something I can help you with. Perhaps if you took a closer look at your punishment, you may remember. All punishments relate to the sins souls committed when they were alive.' Niamh turned back to Caius as tears formed in Eoghan's eyes. 'Please come with me, Caius. It's your time.'

Caius took a step towards Niamh before turning back to Eoghan.

'I'm sorry,' said Caius. 'There's nothing I can do, and I don't want to be stuck here for a thousand years.'

'No,' said Eoghan, raising his eyes to meet Caius's. 'No, you don't.' Tears began to fall from his eyes. He had finally got to meet Death and she wouldn't take him on to the next world. He was going to be alone again.

'Remember what she said,' said Caius. 'Good luck, Eoghan.' With that, Caius turned back to Niamh, and together they walked into the distant fog, fading away into Tír na nÓg.

Eoghan closed his eyes as hot tears flowed swiftly down his face. Taking a deep, snivelling breath, he reopened them and saw the emptiness that surrounded him. More than ever, he felt the pang of loneliness. He had only spent a few hours with Caius, but the man had been the only light in the darkness of the past thousand years. He already missed him. Why couldn't he remember his sin?

Eoghan swallowed, lay down on the road and closed his eyes. He knew he'd regret it when he woke, but his loneliness was tearing a new hole in his chest. After a few deep breaths, the Celtic warrior drifted off into a sleep and dreamed again. He wanted to dream of his family; of his village, of the dirt roads and the rolling hills of green that surrounded his home.

Instead, Eoghan was greeted by a room which seemed familiar, but he couldn't quite place. It was dark and cool; the only light in the room was moonlight dripping through a small hole in the thatch. This wasn't a dream he could control, he realised. It was a memory, it was his sin. Even with the moonlight, he couldn't see very well, but the living warrior knew exactly where he was going. He found his way to a heavy wooden door and released the iron fastening with the strength of a solider. Eoghan pulled open the door. He couldn't see what was inside, but he could hear the desperate, terrified whimpers of the one who resided inside: Eoghan's personal prisoner.

He

Katherine Hackett

I would draw him in straight black lines,
Neat and bold, his eyes warning signs,
Picture-perfect skin, without a scar
or blemish in his whitewashed photo,
With eyes of charcoal and skin of snow,
His chiaroscuro flesh and blood hidden
beneath his spilled-ink suit, forbidden
and foreboding, all stoicism and poise,
His mouth seems to speak white noise,
Until a smile cracks that paper face,
And diffuses colour through the space,
Pink swoops through the black and white,
He flushes, eyes wide and bright,
Laughter sends aqua down his chin,
Yellow sunbursts streak his skin,
Auburn-smudged hair to highlight,
The dye brushed through his sight,
Eyes framed by strands of russet and wine,
I would paint him soft, in seams of sunshine.

No Guts, No Glory

Jenny Nguyen

FADE IN:

INT. UNDERGROUND WAREHOUSE - NIGHT

Grimy walls. Bright lights.

GAME SHOW MUSIC PLAYS. AUDIENCE CHEERS.

HOST (30s) strides onstage and tweaks his mic.
In an immaculate white suit, he has the air of a
ringmaster with a hunger to please his audience.

>   HOST
> Now, before the break, contestant
> 366 lost to 767...

AUDIENCE AWS. He pouts.

>   HOST (CONT'D)
> Which means we'll have to say
> bye-bye to 366, and --

A CLOWN HORN HONKS. Confetti bursts from above.

THE AUDIENCE OOHS. Host gasps excitedly.

>   HOST (CONT'D)
> You know what that sound means,
> right, ladies and gentlemen?

>   AUDIENCE
> Bloodshed! Bloodshed!

He laughs and takes out a golden ENVELOPE from his
inside pocket. He opens it.

>   HOST
> This week's wildcard punishment
> for the loser is...

DRUM ROLL PLAYS.

> HOST (CONT'D)
> From our canine friends!

366 (40s), a greasy pudgy man, is on his hands and knees clutching his chest - he finds it hard to breathe. Blood dribbles from his mouth.

ADAM (30s), also known as 767, stands beside him, wiping his busted lip. Dressed in a grubby shirt, he's a good guy in a bad situation who's fighting. Constantly fighting.

366 grabs Adam's arm.

> 366
> What the hell does that mean?

> ADAM
> I-I don't know.

TWO MASKED MEN grab 366 and push him off the stage into the pit. He falls to his knees.

> 366
> What's happening? What's going to
> happen to me?

Host grins at him.

> HOST
> My darlings must be starving.

Metal doors open revealing a pack of growling hunting DOGS.

366 turns and scurries away but trips over strewn bones.

The dogs encircle him, saliva drips from their jaws.

> 366
> P-Please! Please help me!

Adam takes a step forward but hesitates.

                    HOST
          Eat.

366 makes a run towards the other side. A dog
pounces, bites on his leg and thrashes around,
tearing off flesh, devouring him.

He screams in agony.

THE AUDIENCE LAUGHS. An AUDIENCE MEMBER holds up
THEATRE GLASSES for a better look.

Adam watches, eyes wide, mouth open, his hand
slightly outstretches toward what's left of 366 -
he's horrified.

Host kisses his fingertips and throws his hand in
the air.

                    HOST (CONT'D)
          Bellissimo!

He jumps down into the pit, kneels on one knee and
opens his arms. The dogs run towards him. Adam
shuts his eyes and turns away.

Host giggles (O.S.).

Adam opens his eyes in surprise.

The dogs lick Host, tails wagging, smearing blood
on his face, staining his white suit.

                    HOST (CONT'D)
          Give it up for our darlings!

AUDIENCE CHEERS.

                    HOST (CONT'D)
          We'll be back after the break with
          767 in the last round to see who
          will win an organ of their choice,
          and a bonus of $5,000,000!

AUDIENCE APPLAUDS. GAME SHOW MUSIC PLAYS.

INT. BATHROOM - NIGHT

Adam bursts through the door, drops to his knees and vomits in the toilet.

He breathes heavily, his head in his hands.

He wipes his chin and reaches for his back pocket.

He takes out his WALLET, and opens it to reveal a PHOTO - a bald YOUNG GIRL (14) beaming. He caresses the photo with his thumb, shuts his eyes and sighs.

He flushes the toilet, walks to the sink, rinses his mouth and splashes his face with water.

A FIGURE walks up beside him. The lights flicker.

                    HOST
          Quite a bloodshed out there,
          wasn't it?

Adam looks up at him through the mirror. Host grins, revealing blood on his teeth.

He rolls up his blood-stained sleeves and washes his hands. The water turns red.

Adam wipes his wet hands on his trousers.

                    ADAM
          Was there really a need for that?

                    HOST
          All contestants enter of their own
          accord.

He shrugs, takes out a COMB from his inside pocket, wets it under the tap, and combs the sides of his hair.

                    ADAM
          No one died in the previous
          rounds. They all went through that
          weird metal door. So why him?

Host rubs his teeth with a finger and makes a toothy grin in the mirror. He clicks his tongue.

                    HOST
          Going through that door is
          probably worse than what happened
          to 366.

                    ADAM
          His name is John.

                    HOST
          366, John - same thing. Does it
          even matter now?

Adam grabs Host's shirt and slams him against the
wall.

                    ADAM
          Don't talk about him that way.

Host snorts.

                    HOST
          Seriously? You just competed
          against him.

Adam looks around, trying to find the right words.

                    ADAM
          No one was supposed to die.

                    HOST
          I'm the host. I know what's needed
          to make a great show.

He leans forward, but Adam shoves him back. Host
sighs.

                    ADAM
          What you're doing here with
          people... It's not right.

                    HOST
          And what? Will you leave?

Adam lowers his eyes. Host pouts.

                    HOST (CONT'D)
          Of course, what about poor LILY?

Adam's grip tightens. Host grins.

                  ADAM
        How do you know about her?

Host ignores him.

                  HOST
        You're bound by paper, 767. Just
        like the rest of the world.

                  ADAM
        Don't you dare touch her.

Host rolls his eyes before staring at him.

                  HOST
        Quite unusual... for a contestant
        to win for someone else.

He reaches for the paper towel to dry his hands.

                  HOST (CONT'D)
        366 wasn't just a drug lord, but
        also a leader of a ring which
        forced girls into work.

He picks a speck of dust off his sleeve.

                  HOST (CONT'D)
        Girls as young as your Lily.

Adam's grip loosens.

                  HOST (CONT'D)
        He needed a new heart after all
        that drug abuse, and the money to
        keep business going.

Host looks at Adam carefully. He leans in closer.

                  HOST
        Feeling better, 767?

No response.

Host laughs. He nods.

>   HOST
>   Hmm... well. You're the one who
>   needs something from me, so if
>   you'd like to-

He gestures to Adam's hold. Adam lets go
reluctantly.

>   HOST (CONT'D)
>   Now, if you'll excuse me, I have
>   to go for a costume change. Red's
>   really not my colour.

He straightens out his jacket, salutes Adam and
strides out the door. Adam stares at the blood on
his hands.

INT. UNDERGROUND WAREHOUSE - NIGHT

DRUM ROLL PLAYS. Host rubs his hands together.

>   HOST
>   Now what you've been waiting for!
>   Get ready to place your bets!

The doors open revealing two masked men dragging a
FIGURE by the arms, their legs brush against the
ground.

Adam turns to watch.

The audience goes wild and throws cash from the
balconies. The figure lifts his head.

Adam's expression turns into disbelief.

INT. POLICE OFFICE - DAY [FLASHBACK]

CHIEF Lewis (50s) slams a FILE on his desk.

>   CHIEF
>   You've left me with no choice.

Adam rubs his bloodshot eyes, scratches his
unshaven beard.

>   CHIEF (CONT'D)
>   It's been four years.

                    ADAM
          He's my friend —

                    CHIEF
          The body was found - case closed.

                    ADAM
          The body isn't his! It's-

He stops abruptly, sways a little. Chief Lewis
sighs.

                    CHIEF
          Not this again, Adam. The team
          can't deal with you like this.
          He leans forward in his chair.

                    CHIEF (CONT'D)
          It's interfering with your work.

Adam shakes his head.

                    ADAM
          I need this job. You know that,
          Chief. You know about my problems.

                    CHIEF
          I'm sorry, but it's not an excuse.
          I'm letting you go, Adam.

Adam shakes his head in disbelief before storming
out.

Chief Lewis sighs and rubs his neck. He picks up
the FILE, looks at it, and throws it back down
again.

A PHOTO is attached to the FILE with a name -
MARCUS Hunt.

INT. UNDERGROUND WAREHOUSE - NIGHT [PRESENT]

The two masked men throw the figure into the pit.

                    ADAM
          ... Mark?

Marcus (30s), a steely-eyed scrawny guy, holds his side and groans in pain.

> ADAM (CONT'D)
> Marcus!

Marcus looks up, squints at the bright lights, but then sees Adam. His eyes widen.

The curtains behind Host lifts to reveal a GAME WHEEL.

> HOST
> We'll let fate decide, shall we?

He reaches up to pull down the lever. The GAME WHEEL spins.

Adam's eyes tear up as he stares at Marcus.

Marcus stares back, his jaw clenches.

The GAME WHEEL slows - all eyes are on it. It stops.

> HOST (CONT'D)
> Blind man's bluff!

THE AUDIENCE ERUPTS IN CHEERS. Host grins.

> HOST (CONT'D)
> The object of the game is simple:
> don't get caught, or you'll be it.

The doors open, revealing IT (20s) resting a FLAIL on his shoulder, wearing a blindfold.

Adam takes a step back. Marcus smirks.

A BUZZER SOUNDS.

> HOST (CONT'D)
> May the best man win.

It darts forward, swinging the FLAIL over his head.

Adam ducks, runs to the other side tripping over

the bones. Marcus slams him into the wall, Adam's head takes a hit.

THE AUDIENCE OOHS. Adam groans in pain, clutching his bleeding head.

> ADAM
> Mark, what the fu-

> MARCUS
> The name's 343.

It darts towards them, swinging the FLAIL at their heads. They jump away just in time, the FLAIL cracks the wall.

> MARCUS (CONT'D)
> I'm gonna fucking win this time.

Marcus picks up a BONE off the floor and aims for Adam. They tumble, a mass of limbs trying to get the upper hand.

Marcus lands on top, pushes the BONE against Adam's neck, suffocating him.

Adam claws at Marcus' hands and face, pushing him away.

> ADAM
> Mar- no-

Blood splatters across Adam's face.

Adam looks up, horrified to see half of Marcus' face scraped off before he collapses on top of him.

THE AUDIENCE CHEERS.

It towers over them, his FLAIL drips with blood.

> HOST
> We have a winner!

HALF OF THE AUDIENCE CHEERS, HALF BOOS.

Adam heaves Marcus' body off, breathing heavily. Host tuts.

> HOST (CONT'D)
> Unfortunately, 767 got caught
> which means he'll have to get his
> punishment.

Adam wipes the blood off his face.

> ADAM
> What? Why? I won the prize.

> HOST
> You still got caught. You'll have
> to receive a punishment.

> ADAM
> W-what punishment?

> HOST
> Considering this is blind man's
> bluff... your eyes.

The two masked men grab Adam. He struggles against
them.

> ADAM
> Wait! Get off me! Let me go - I
> fucking won! I need that prize!

Host watches him. He holds up a hand. The masked
men hesitate, the audience quietens.

> HOST
> How about a proposition? One where
> you'll get to keep your eyes?

Adam looks at him hopefully. Host's lips twitch.

> ADAM
> Anything.

> HOST
> You can walk away unharmed...
> with no prize.

Host takes out a SPOON out from his inside pocket,
breathes on it and rubs it against his shoulder.
He taps his eye.

> HOST (CONT'D)
> Or keep the prize and you'll have
> a daughter who lives, but it'll be
> something you'll never get to see.

THE AUDIENCE SHOUT OPTIONS AT ADAM.

ADAM'S POV -- a wild crowd, a sea of frowns,
shaking fists. Cash falls from above, the bright
lights are blinding.

He steps back, an OBJECT catching his eye. He
looks down, seeing his open WALLET with the PHOTO
inside.

He picks it up and hastily wipes off the blood to
reveal Lily's smile.

His shoulders relax, eyes tearing up as he smiles
sadly.

> HOST (CONT'D)
> What will it be, 767?

Adam inhales. He stands.

> ADAM
> I need her to live.

AUDIENCE CHEERS. Host smirks knowingly. The masked
men grab Adam. Host throws the SPOON, the masked
man catches it, and forces Adam on his knees. He
grabs Adam's neck, spoon in hand, nearing his
eyes.

The audience goes wild, cheering and laughing as
they throw money in the pit as Adam screams.

GAME SHOW MUSIC PLAYS AND MUFFLES HIS SCREAMS.

> HOST
> And that's the end of the show,
> ladies and gents! Until next time!

AUDIENCE WHINES. He puts a hand over his heart and
bows.

                    HOST (CONT'D)
          As we say, 'No guts...'

He gestures to the audience.

                    AUDIENCE
          No glory!

The doors open. Host winks and turns. The doors
close.

FADE OUT.

New Orthodox Culture

J Mann

flowers sold their
colour to the old
oligarch of selfish lane
'twas never the same

life starred people into
constellations of
picture-perfect stickers
inside a melting heart flickers

dreams advertise
lives to the wide eyed
Google left cookies
on the table side

weather coloured
their brains whilst
soil comforted
the feet pained rains

buried standing up stars
implanted into tiles
tombstones disguised as
life stone miles

somebody's sold
a magazine to the
self-conscious zebra,
No good news for a Libra

beasts chasing roads
down the motorway
gawking stand the toads
wishing themselves astray

darling of the nation
she is wedded to
sensation
subject to inflation

pet humans are
waiting for lives in
digital cages with
No pre or post ages

The Ramblas

Alan Mahar

He was following the dry paths towards the *ramblas*. It might have been that he had nowhere to be. He knew no one here apart from Angie, who had her work during the day, and Natalie at school, but they would be at their own apartment later, a safe distance away. She hadn't encouraged his visit: impromptu wasn't helpful, she said, even if he was having problems back in England. This morning, he had decided, he may as well be on the look-out for birdlife. A relief to be away from the white-walled villas and the blue-tiled pools of the so-called *urbanizacion*. Ahead might be a little owl bopping into a burrow in the high clay banks of the river; or before Gerry reached the trickle of the measly water, the possibility of a mask-faced shrike in a fig tree. He only wanted the chance to talk to her properly and explain. Already a hoopoe was making a rattling whoop in the under-growth before it took fright and skittered away.

There were a few other people up early and trudging the paths: in the distance by an electricity pylon a man with two spaniels; closer to the road a woman with a black Labrador. Probably Brits. They both seemed to dissolve into the scrub the closer he approached. He passed no one and faced no one oncoming to say 'good morning' to in English. He thought he saw a dog on its own, it wasn't a fox, but a grey skulking mutt of some sort, surely not a greyhound, disappearing away.

Gerry had advanced beyond the recently halted construction of the golf course/hotel complex, which was still no more than a mess of fences and concrete stumps. He faced the dry hills, and beyond them more hills, all part of the coastal sierra. The two peaks of the *Espuña*, a wildlife conservation area, where wild boar and horned mountain sheep roamed free, dominated the horizon to the north. An observation post, cordoned off for military purposes, on one summit; the other unspoiled, circled, he was told, by soaring eagles. To one side a hill town, Totana, where buildings clustered round the steep top. Below the *Espuña* miles of arable plain, and a market town at Alhama. He hoped he was beginning to orient himself better with each day.

The day before he had taken a bus trip to the next big town, Lorca, where medieval Muslims had occupied the area peaceably and only been quashed and driven out by the church-mad Spaniards. He read about the peaceable Moorish settlement and their infiltration across this dry land. Then what Franco did to the country; graves were still being unearthed. But in a town square there he had seen small groups of Ecuadorians gathered at the roadside, browner than the pale native complexion, with more layers of colourful clothes than the Spaniards. They stood half in the street, impassive, not speaking; Gerry wondered if he was expected to offer them money. They would be hoping to be hired again, to pick vegetables from under the field-sized roofs of plastic sheeting.

No one in their right mind strolled the dry paths, except for the few English settlers on the *urbanizacion* who kept their dogs with them in Spain. The moment they left behind the straight lines of bright-painted villas, white walls and terracotta roofs, they were thrown into a comforting wilderness of rough grass and weeds, shrubs and thistles. Gerry felt a freedom from the villa it had been arranged for him to stay in, and especially, he thought, from the chill of its shiny floor.

He headed for the *ramblas*, the strip of land where the river was meant to be. Over the scrub leading to the hillside plantations of regimented almond and olives it was encouraging to see low greener bushes, woody rosemary, juniper; they hugged the curves of the *ramblas* for moisture. There were even little copses in the bend of the river, where he might hope for some stirrings of birdlife.

He had to be wary of straying on to farmland property with a Spanish landowner intolerant of foolish English exiles, ignorant of local laws, out in the countryside walking their dogs, with no genuine (farming) reason for being there. Gerry passed a sign he only half understood warning against hunting: *cani y cecca vieto*. The bulky rabbits scuttling in the scrub were long and meaty, twice the size of British rabbits, almost as big as hares, but not nearly so streamlined for speed. They were so numerous he could almost see the point of hunting them. The green and red plastic cartridges strewn on the bankside, next to sheltering bushes for hunters, must have been for rabbit meat, unless intended for the red-legged partridges, or the mallard dabbling in the meagre river pools. Angie said she heard shooting some nights. It had frightened her at first. But it was only illegal hunters. The Spanish had their own rules and laws. Some locals took their chances, seeing the shooting as a right forbidden only to foreign settlers. They must have felt entitled to their own rabbits for the stew pot. He could offer to cook something else for her and Natalie, if she would let him.

On the opposite high bank he peered through the perimeter fence of a pig farm that stretched up the hill for miles. Pigeons and finches balanced on the wire. Across the hillside the pigs ranged free, comparatively free, freer, happier, he expected, than in the metal pen of an English factory farm. The creatures were always close to their designated shelter and trough, contented enough for fattening and farrowing. A quad-bike bounced around the field and replenished the feeding troughs. The pigs pottered around their corrugated iron shelters. Their companionable noises – a baby's squeal, a liquid cry, a tubercular cough or a long snore – carried right across the distance to his side of the *ramblas*. Gerry overheard their family's noises as if he was hearing voices in a radio drama. The friendly sounds made him think more fondly of the bacon in his *bocadillo*, the *jamon* on his plate of *Iberico*. The Spanish, whom he didn't pretend to understand the way Angie was starting to since she had moved here, treated these animals with consideration. He would have some ground to make up.

Deeper into the hillocks of the scrubland, where the paths began to turn more, a large skinny greyish dog was trotting in front of him. It was the lurcher, sparse-haired, rangy and loping along, confident but also nervous of any approach. Gerry realised it was ownerless, wandering alone, a dog with a manky coat. The animal kept his distance but still looked back. If Gerry approached, the dog trotted further off. In no particular hurry, not frightened, but still it was an animal that was wary. With its steady trot onwards and away along the uneven path it somehow managed to present the impression of purpose to Gerry. He could manage on his own. There was enough space to roam; he could hunt. He was a running dog, and this open land was his natural habitat. Equally, he could curl up on anyone's sofa and make himself at home, if allowed. He only wanted to be taken in hand and set a task. He wouldn't interfere with livestock. He was loyal and well-intentioned, Gerry could see that. The lurcher stopped in front of a tall rosemary bush and stared back at Gerry as if to question what a human was doing wandering the scrubland.

Gerry stopped too; and disturbed a crested lark from the rough grass, causing it to lift a few feet up, brown, short-tailed and flapping with sudden annoyance. A noisy show of wings and chirping in the air above them and the bird wheeled over to settle safely on a tussock a little way off, its crest raised; it seemed confident it would re-find its resting place and resettle itself.

The lark distracted him. He would need to sit down with Angie for a proper conversation.

The dog turned its grey shoulder, trotted away up the incline towards the outbuildings of the goat farm further across the hillside. He would present himself to them at the yard, arrive uninvited, serve himself up, hoping for acceptance, if not a home then temporary asylum. He would solicit the kind of firm sympathy a dog requires: for someone to make him useful again, give him the chance to be truly a lurcher again, the type of dog he was, which he couldn't help being, it was his breed, and here he was in this place.

The Woodwards
Derek Littlewood

If this tree could speak, what should it say for you?
– Jochen Gerz

woodwords willed
a gust of wind
   as leaflets left
to float fleeting
   sudden scuffle
in midland hawthorn
   black bryony laced
as last light lingers
   green woodpecker
in dipping flight
   bitter-sweet berries
burn tartly on
   leaflitter on leaving
step sheer into
   Forest where
darkening onset
   as November sun
ash arches across
   face ducked down
ringed round
   birch beech become
overstepping understory
   no colours now
vixen, weasel chatter

willow glow
in yellow glade
   brown branches
through mild air
   crowchatter caw
hazel hedge
   nuts squirreled away
in woodland glade
   would yaffle over
dropping into dusk.
   burnished nightshade
fool's tongue; spit into
   the lighted clearing
Worcestershire's Wyre
   bear boar & hart roamed.
landgulls leaving
   sinks sudden
the way now
   through oak groves
with small leaved lime
   vast chestnut boles
to the heartwood
   nightbarks of fox
and owl screech

    ahead brock's barrow
a dank ditch
    charcoal's burnt
ring of fire & stone
    through miasma
hushed voices singing,
    whistle fiddle & flute
echo in forest shade
    swelling to a dark hum
reek of fungi fumes
    rats running
trespasser torn
    ahead Jack in
the furzy man
    Woodwose waiting
wilderwood bewildered

    bars the way
& bank where
    blackened fern fronds
earth clamp smoking
    moving through the air
shimmering bells
    jigs & reels surge & fade
sway of sounds
    thrumming now through
woods creeping round
    trees turn traitor
roots trip, twigs clutch
    the Green gathers,
face beleaved, a
    on the woodway
be wilded here.

Glass

Kay Flax

I was already two glasses into a bottle of Pinot when Leigh got home. An elaborately carved bottle empty of Amaretto lay at my feet. Splinters of eyeliner shavings scattered the vanity. Leigh's curling tongs were burning at 230 degrees, dangerously close to the tissue paper poking out of the gift bag I'd arranged for her two days before. Several of Leigh's necklaces lay tangled in a glittering knot at my elbow. Mine – the one I'd planned to wear – sat pretty in its velvet box, showered with rubbish, in the bin. A thin layer of matte powder coated my mirror – but I was entirely put together. Not a hair out of place.

Leigh was too busy motor-mouthing to notice the disorder. 'I'm late, I know, I'm late. The thing is, work needed me to finish a display, then on my way out I got stopped by this Big Issue seller, though I don't think she was actually selling the Big Issue because her satchel thing was clunking in a way magazines don't, and I was like, lady, you need to get out of the doorway, my manager will screw! And I only got away when I shoved her off on Josie, because I am not paid enough to deal with that crap, right? And I started to run for the tube, but then I felt like I was sweating, and I knew I wouldn't have time to shower, so I had to walk – and anyway, you can't be mad if we're late to something I'm dragging you to, right? Oh my god.' I heard it in her voice, when Leigh finally noticed our surroundings. I heard it in the thud of her bag hitting the floor. 'Gwen? Are you okay?'

'You're late.' I pushed myself from the vanity. The bottle of honeyed vanilla perfume Leigh bought me for my birthday wobbled and lost to gravity, landing on the delicate edges of its glass-rose lid. 'You'd better get ready. Sort your hair. It's a mess.'

But she followed me out of the room and into the kitchen, tripping over her bag in the process. 'Gwen? What's going on? What happened to your room?'

'I was in a rush.'

'And the wine?'

'I got the party started early.'

'And this?' I turned to see her holding the empty Amaretto bottle. 'This isn't sold in Waitrose, Gwen. Blake and I bought it in Italy!'

'Over a year ago.'

'Celebrating our anniversary!'

'And it's been clogging up the kitchen since.'

Leigh stopped still in the doorway, blocking me in. She slammed the bottle down next to the microwave. 'What the hell is wrong with you?'

The fact that she had no idea just made it worse. She didn't know, and it shouldn't be on me to tell her.

'We're late. Fix your eyeliner, you're drooping. And if you're planning on wearing what's draped over your mirror, pick again.'

'I asked you a question.'

'And I booked a taxi for 7:45. You need to get ready.'

Leigh's eyes flickered to the clock on the microwave. 7:27. 'Fine. Tell me in the taxi. And for the love of god, don't have anything else to drink.'

She rushed off to her bedroom. I threw the Amaretto bottle into the recycling bin and opened a fresh bottle of wine.

The taxi ride was a grind – house music over a tinny car radio, the overpowering smell of false pine, beads on the driver's seat cover clacking with every sudden slam of the brake. But it peaked when Leigh turned to me, so close I could smell the eggs she'd had for lunch, and said, 'Right, are you gonna tell me what's eating at you, so we can get it out and enjoy the night?'

'You didn't have time to clean your teeth?'

She huffed and dug through her bag, coming up with apple bubble-gum that did nothing to disguise the smell. And then she looked at me, chewing, expectant.

I said nothing.

'You slept badly?' she guessed. 'You couldn't get on the cross trainer at the gym? Work made you answer emails on the weekend? You got stuck in an overcrowded tube on the way to the jewellers?'

I felt my face twitch.

'The jewellers? Okay. You got to the jewellers, but they'd screwed up your necklace? They hadn't fixed it at all? They lost it? Well? Did you get it back or not?'

'I got it back.'

'But you're not happy with it? Look, just tell Blake. He can speak to his manager, get them to fix it properly. You probably won't even have to pay. Why didn't you tell him there and then? Did you get his employee discount? Did you even see him?'

Yes, Leigh, I saw him. I deliberately went when you said he'd be on his lunch break, but I caught him coming back from it. Literally caught him.

'Well? Did you see him?'

'I saw him.'

'But he didn't give you his discount? Is that why you're mad? For god's sake, will you please just spit it out?'

I would not. Blake had been chewing her up and spitting her out for years anyway. It was his to do, one last time.

'All right, if you won't tell me, fine. Just don't sit there prickly and on edge all night. My aunt already thinks you're a snob, after Christmas.'

'Your aunt's cook-from-frozen *prawn medley* gave me food poisoning!'

'Well, Blake too, but he's not holding it against her.'

'No, Blake has other things to hold on to.' It was out before I could stop it.

Leigh turned to look at me. 'What's that supposed to mean?'

I wanted to unleash it all. The jewellers, the confrontation, the pleading phone call. The frustration that boiled into a rage that trashed my bedroom and destroyed all his guilt-provoked gifts. I could have told her.

I didn't.

I stared at the car window, pretending I could see out of it, saying nothing.

'Okay, whatever. You've got a strop on because you didn't want to come tonight – don't take it out on me, okay? You didn't have to come.'

No. I didn't. And up until that afternoon, I'd had no intention of going. But that phone call hadn't left Blake in the best of moods, either – and I would sooner Leigh be frustrated with my mood, sooner her whole family think I was a snob, than have her face that without me.

Leigh sighed. 'The Almighty Silent Gwen. What a great night we're in for.'

Like she had any idea.

'It's our little Leelee! Oh, look at you. Do a twirl, Leigh. Give Auntie Barb a twirl.'

Every time. Leigh's aunt treats Leigh like a two-year-old – and, so desperate to please, Leigh happily regresses to that age, loving the attention. On cue, she laughed and spun on the spot, her dress whirling around her.

I could have screamed. *You are twenty-five! You shouldn't be wearing a dress you bought online from a 'Cartoon Couture' collection, you shouldn't want to look like a Powerpuff Girl, and you definitely shouldn't be twirling like a toddler in an Easter bonnet parade! Grow up!*

'Such a beautiful young lady!' Leigh's aunt said; and then, the sugar on her tongue turning to flour, added, 'Oh. You brought Gwen. That's nice. But where's Blake? He's coming, isn't he?'

Saint Blake, The Pensioner's Friend. Drank their tea and pretended the powdered milk tasted nice, carried their shopping, smarmed his way in until they thought he was marriage material, because they never dreamed of what he did when Leigh wasn't around.

'He's meeting us here. He had to work late.'

Yes. Work. That was exactly what he did at that wretched jewellers. *Worked* with his colleagues.

Leigh's aunt clucked her tongue. 'Poor thing. Such a hard worker. But he'll go far, he will – he's got the gift of the gab, our Blake, could sell ice to an Eskimo. Well, come and do the rounds! Everybody wants to see you.' Her bony fingers gripped Leigh's arm, pearlescent pink nails resting against Leigh's skin. Leigh looked back at me, as hesitant to leave as her aunt was to have me follow. 'Oh, don't worry about Gwen. She'll get the drinks in, won't you, Gwen?'

Leigh opened her mouth to argue, but I cut her off with a smile as falsely sweet as her aunt's. 'What a good idea.' And I made my way to the bar.

For a function room in a social club, where beer mats were still fashionable and the wood was two shades too dark to be modern, the bar staff were awfully picky about who they served. Maybe Leigh's aunt had got to them, warned them that I was a snob; because they ignored me, serving Worthington's and sherry to her decrepit old friends while I waited long past my turn. If they'd addressed the bar in order, I wouldn't have still been standing there when Blake arrived, making a beeline for the bar before even acknowledging Leigh. Through the mirror on the back of the bar, with its peeling decals of 80s beer advertisements, I watched him sidle over, so close the short sleeves of his obnoxiously patterned shirt brushed against my shoulder.

'Getting the drinks in, Gwendoline? Surprised you came. Thought Leigh's family functions literally made you sick.'

'What makes me sick is you talking to me like nothing's changed.'

'Careful, Gwyneth,' he said, throwing his arm around me. His touch felt toxic. 'We agreed to act civil tonight, remember.'

I shunted my shoulder, trying to get free of his arm. 'No, you wanted to act civil. Clearly to give yourself time to think your way out-'

'What do you want me to do? Upset her in front of her family?'

'Right. God forbid they learn what a scumbag you really are.'

'Look on the bright side,' he said, signalling a bartender with his free hand. She nodded at him, as if I hadn't been waiting nearly fifteen minutes. 'You get to be smug for a few more hours, knowing you've got a proper reason to hate me at last. I'll have a Carling, please, love. Gwenny? Drink?'

The bartender finally acknowledged me with a reluctant cock of her head, but I shoved Blake's arm off and walked away.

From a table on the edge of the room, away from nosy pensioners and paper plates of frozen gateaux and gristly sausage rolls, I watched Blake. Watched him find Leigh and sling an arm around her shoulder, swigging from his pint while she looked dotingly up at him. Watched him dance with Leigh's aunt and her friends like there was nothing he'd rather do than 'YMCA' with aging women. Watched him growing drunker, louder; less charming, more rowdy. Watched Leigh change as Blake did – her posture stiffening, her smile growing tight. Watched her convince him to go out for fresh air. Watched him leaning on her to walk a straight line.

Her family laughed it off. *Boys will be boys*. And in that minute, I could see it all – could *smell* the flowers he'd buy the next day to worm his way back into Leigh's good graces. Pretty flowers and prettier lies.

So when they walked outside, I followed.

Leigh propped Blake against the wall of the club. He slumped, swirling the last dregs in his glass; she stood opposite him, shivering slightly. My breath came out in little clouds that drifted closer to them, away from the shadowy recess of the building where I skulked, unseen.

Leigh broke the silence, her voice excessively chirpy. 'It's cold out here.'

'Could've stayed inside.'

'I just thought you needed some fresh air. You've had a lot to drink.'

'It's a party, Leigh.'

Leigh hesitated. 'We should probably call it a night. Are you alright staying here, if I go find Gwen?'

Blake laughed. It was harsh, unamused. 'Surprised she didn't follow us out. You and Gwen, always tied arse to cheek.'

Leigh sighed. 'Please don't start.'

'She's had it in for me from the beginning.'

'That's not true.'

Yes, it is.

'Yeah it is. She hated that you had something she didn't.'

No. She hated that you made Leigh stupid and spineless.

'Come on, she-'

'Can't stand you having someone, because she hasn't got anything herself.'

What she *has* is responsibility for Leigh – because when she slips, Leigh makes decisions like being with you.

'That's not fair-'

'Not fair is not being able to see your girlfriend without a third wheel!'

'Oh, that's rich, you talking about third wheels.' I walked out of the shadows, and Blake stood up straight. No more tipsy slump; all bravado and arrogance, like my presence had stirred it to the surface.

'Here she is. Never far behind, are you, Gwenbo?'

'What happened to being civil, Blake?'

'Ooh, there's that biting wit. All talk and no walk, aren't you?'

All talk.

All talk. Like he hadn't pleaded with me, swearing it was a goodbye kiss, the whole thing a mistake. Like he hadn't begged me to let him be the one to tell Leigh. Persuaded me to give him one more day, because it meant giving Leigh one more night to be happy.

Leigh glanced between us. 'Gwen? Blake? What's going on?'

'Well, Gwenny? Anything you want to share with the group?'

He was so confident I wouldn't say a word. So sure he was safe.

'Tell Leigh just how into sharing you are, Blake.'

Blake stared me down.

'Tell her how hard all those extra hours at work have been.'

'Oh, Gwyneth. Always with the dramatics-'

'Tell her how close you've got to your colleagues. Tell her all about your team-building exercises.'

'Blake? What's going on? What does she mean?'

'She doesn't know what she's talking about, Leigh-'

'Tell her what I know. What I saw.'

Leigh moved – shifted, just slightly – away from Blake. Closer to me.

I held out my hand.

She took it.

'What did Gwen see, Blake?'

'Leigh. Come back. She's just trying to stir the pot-'

'Was it *her*?' She reeled on me. 'What did you see, Gwen?'

'"Her"?' I asked. 'What have *you* seen? What do *you* know?'

She faltered.

'Leigh, none of it is what you think it is. Just calm down, hear me out-'

'Oh, by all means, Blake, speak! Tell her all about your

redheaded colleague. Tell her!'

But Leigh – oblivious, in the dark, blissfully unaware Leigh – said: '*Redheaded* colleague?'

She stared at him, frozen, as the implication settled over the three of us.

I asked, 'Exactly how many girls are there, Blake?'

But he couldn't answer me. He was just as still as Leigh, like one more word might crack his whole world open.

'One less, now,' Leigh said.

Blake's glass hit the concrete and smashed.

Sewers

Lucy Farrington-Smith

eyes down,
i'm there:
by the
sewer –
side by
side with
myself –
selfish
girl, you
ran and
you fell –

eyes down,
i'm there:
don't look –
it's
painless
and this
is quick –
a drop
from the
storm on
hellbent
eyes –
the rain
always
falls, and
so have
i –

eyes down,
i'm there:
spitting
blood from
my lips –
it's not
quick, they
lied – i
still feel,
i feel
i feel
it all –
just let
me
go – eyes
down, i'm
there, i'm
there, i –

Watcher in the Night

Sophie Ludgate

The night is dark, but I see everything.

I see the once pure earth soaking up the vermillion aftermath, revelling in it.

It's getting hungry and you're feeding it, all of you. And you care, or you did.

It's just a job, right?

Maybe, if you think it hard enough, you'll start to believe it.

Then you can sleep at night.

You watch the shadows dance as the people cower and you think, *it's for my country*.

The people – you have to stop calling them people.

One of them, brave or cowardly? He surrenders, hands up, protecting.

You should give him mercy, but I see you, your finger slowly curling around that cold metal trigger.

I see the bullet carve its way through the air and make contact with smooth tanned flesh.

He falls to the ground and that hungry earth rejoices.

Aortic spray. Lovely.

Do you feel big now?

He liked to sing.

You brought a man to his knees and now he'll never sing again.

This isn't a war. It's an execution.

Equation of Time
Bonnie Cartwright

"When I Do Count The Clock That Tells The Time."
- Shakespeare's *Sonnet 12*.

Luminous cyclops of morning sunshine
jerking the shadow out from under her
and then fetching it back: a creeping thing,
a roaming that turns the hours of stillness ––
she is the arbor and sundial in this,
her Garden of Eden and lavender.
The wet clunking of the tank inside her ––
the wheezing release. The softest dry hum.
It stinks of Gold Leaf and peppermint oil.

The grass is long here: spiny tubes probing
the sweat-slick knees, creaking hips, hammered toes.
Her horology now turned retrograde,
Linear –– the roses wilted early.
Hands open. Visitation is yearly.

Notes on the Contributors

Ali AElsey is a singer-songwriter, poet, author and founder of the writing group "Budding Writers". She is preparing a short story collection for publication and can often be found reading at assorted pubs and cafes around the West Midlands.

Kate Aspinall is completing her Masters in Creative Writing.

Bonnie Cartwright is currently entering her third year. Driven by a fascination with the 'familiar made strange', she has a weakness for sci-fi and far-off adventures when she isn't wrangling too many pets.

Salma Chowdhury is soon to graduate in BA English. Lost with finding a career for herself she decided to help others find theirs. Aside from the academic world, she works part-time within retail: one of the many places where she finds inspiration in writing heartfelt, family-based screenplays and plays.

Kit de Waal's debut novel, *My Name is Leon* has been shortlisted for various prizes, translated into several languages and optioned for TV and film. She has also won prizes for her short stories and twice won the Bridport Prize for flash fiction. In 2016 she founded a scholarship for marginalised writers.

Lucy Farrington-Smith is a freelance copywriter from Leamington Spa. In her 24 years, she has trained as an actor, toured the UK with a theatre company, and worked in advertising, producing marketing materials for trucks and tractors. She currently maintains a fashion and lifestyle blog, and regularly contributes to The Huffington Post.

Rhiannon Fidler is a writer based in the Midlands, usually Birmingham or Northampton. She grew up in villages surrounded by musicians and singers but decided to stick to poetry when she figured out she couldn't sing.

Kay Flax has been writing since the age of twelve, when she wrote her first 'novel' in alternating colours of felt-tip pen. Fascinated by the intricacies of relationships, she still spends far too much time talking herself out of typing in rainbow colours.

Rhoda Greaves is a Lecturer in Creative Writing in the School of English, and an Associate Editor of Short Fiction journal. 'Mackerel for Tea' was long-listed in the Bristol Short Story Prize (2012), shortlisted in Aesthetica's Creative Writing Competition (2014), and first published in Aesthetica's Creative Writing Anthology (2014). You can follow her on Twitter @ rhodagreaves.

Katherine Hackett is a writer of poetry and fiction. Also known as Katie, Kat, Katlou or Jeremy, she's written as many as two thousand first drafts and has begun a second. She enjoys reading and reading.

Leila Howl has a penchant for weird worlds and unusual characters, writing speculative fiction and scripts for screen and radio. She can be found on Twitter @lkhowl_writing, and blogs about writing, gaming and parenting at lkhowlwriting.wordpress.com and babyledgeek.wordpress.com.

Shazmeen Khalid is a second-year English student and has been writing for over five years, sharing her poetry via her blog. Through her writing she grapples with her polarised identity. *Tongues* demonstrates a modern and mature slice of a multicultural writer's work and shows the difficulty of claiming one's heritage when writing and speaking in a colonised tongue.

Gregory Leadbetter's poetry collections include *The Fetch* (Nine Arches Press, 2016) and the pamphlet *The Body in the Well* (HappenStance, 2007). His book *Coleridge and the Daemonic Imagination* (Palgrave Macmillan, 2011) won the University English Book Prize 2012. He is Director of both the MA in Creative Writing and the Institute of Creative and Critical Writing at Birmingham City University, where he is Reader in Literature and Creative Writing. www.gregoryleadbetter.blogspot.co.uk

Joe Legge has just finished his final year of Creative Writing with English.

Derek Littlewood teaches literature and creative writing in the School of English. He lives in Worcestershire with his family and is a keen naturalist. His next poetry project will be called *Crypto* and will explore the overlap of the virtual and urban worlds.

His work was longlisted in the National Poetry Competition 2016. http://www.dereklittlewood.com/

Sophie Ludgate writes everything from flash fiction to novels, and has had short stories published in both the US and UK. She currently lives in Birmingham where she's completing her MA in Creative Writing.

Paris Minnett McCalla is studying for an English and Creative Writing degree. Music is her inspiration. She listens to it so much, that she has little time for anything else.

Steve McFall lives in Bournville with his wife Jane, and their children Sam, Ellie and Flo. He has worked as a radio creative all over the UK; career highlights include winning an award with Ghengis Khan selling curtain fabric and being shouted at by Brian Blessed. He has also been a regular contributor to a comedy podcast.

Danny Maguire is a first-year student and a member of the university's writing society, Write Club. He has been telling stories since a young age, from prose to animation to film, and aspires to write novels or screenplays for a living.

Alan Mahar had short stories in *London Magazine, Critical Quarterly* and *Bête Noire,* before his two novels *Flight Patterns* (1998) and *After the Man Before* (2002) were published, and he changed career to become publishing director of the Birmingham fiction publisher, Tindal Street Press (1997-2012).

Jaspinder Mann was born in India and came to England at the age of five. The last three years have ignited an interest in developing an understanding of the relationship between state and society.

Jenny Nguyen is soon to be an English Literature graduate based in Birmingham. Her daydreams are put to good use in her writing as they help to inspire her stories and characters.

Onize Osho weaves dreams and ideas into reality via words. An incorrigible bookworm from childhood, she studied undergraduate law – adding Latin phrases to her lexicon and spice to her prose. Alongside her postgraduate degree Onize is working on a 'magnum opus' (poetry on being human).

David Roberts is Pro Vice Chancellor and Dean of the Faculty of Arts, Design and Media. He is currently working on his thirteenth book, a biography of the Irish dramatist George Farquar. Recent titles include *Restoration Plays and Players* (Cambridge University Press, 2014) and *Games for English Literature* (with Izabela Hopkins, Libri Publishing, 2016). He has also published a novel, *The Life of Harris the Actor,* and writes programme essays for the Royal Opera House.

Esther Withey is about to graduate. A university-led radio workshop gave her a passion for writing scripts involving a strange combination of relationships, psychology and the animal kingdom! She lives in Derby with her husband, where she enjoys casually drawing and fervently knitting.

Alex Woodhouse has written several scripts and is part of a radio writing group run by Helen Cross, which has recorded his drama, *Trapped in Tanks*. He lives in Birmingham and looks to the city for inspiration.